# Rooks of the Raven

Franklin Neal

# Contents

# Prologue

Pa has gone for firewood near the creek. My sister is sleeping and Mama is washing our clothes outside.

When I step out, the wind makes a rough acquaintance. My blouse waves at Mama. The tomatoes are still sour but growing ripe. Mama is hanging the wet clothes. I see Papa's head is bouncing as he carries wood up the small hill.

"Pa, let me help," I say.

He stops chopping wood to glance at me. "Abel." He says my name and that's all.

I already knew he wouldn't want my help. Mama smiled. I walk over to a tree. I climb on a thick branch then slowly lean backward. The leaves rustle and two fall on my hair.

Mama waves me inside, her hair wrapped in a white cloth.

After getting inside, I draw myself a bath. I fill it to the top and dip my head in as if being baptized. If only for a moment, I rinse off the troublesome stains of my life. It feels nice to lie back. The water caresses me—holds me—like I belong.

By the time I get out, the tribe is up. The smell of tea catches my attention. The kettle screams.

"You look alive." Pa says. I notice that Ina is wearing my clothes; we want to share whatever we can with her. Mama and I share one outfit. Pa holds Ina high then starts picking at her like an apple tree. I sit on the sofa, watching. He munches at her toes, then her pushed-out belly button. Ina's eyes are only half open from giggling. He squeezes her nose then spins her around. Ina claps, or better yet, touches her hands together as she is well amused. Mama wipes her hands dry using a small towel with a rip in the center.

The day is great, but of course, Bell was right—there is an emptiness in this home. Mama prepares supper as it has been too long since we enjoyed a well cooked meal as a family. The fragrance of carrots and potatoes swells from the pot. We have greens, corn, and peas. Corn is mixed in the soup with beans on the side, doused in salt and red pepper.

I like salty food, but not too much—just the right amount. I pass out the potatoes that I helped peel. The scratches on the wood table appear deeper than before. I get up and grab the cinnamon. All Mama's spices and seasonings are in old jars. Potatoes and cinnamon go well together.

Ina is making a huge mess, her squishy hands playing in Mama's dish. I wonder if that is how I acted as a child. I enjoy every last bite and go for more. Our tribe's stomachs are full. After supper, I decide to read to Ina. I point at each word as I read Margo's book.

"Pa, did Margo ever read to you when you were with them?" I ask.

"All the time, in secret of course. She even tried to teach me." He laughs. "Mistress tried to teach me, but I lived a different life, hated the world. I didn't care for books. Books are what cast the rooks aside."

"Then I ought to read to you, Pa," I reply. I read a little then toss the book aside.

The candles are dying out, leaving a distinct scent, but a good kind. I only replace the one sitting on a small barrel next to the sofa. Mama joins us.

I'm on the floor. Ina is on my lap wearing clothes three times her size, making me laugh. Mama combs my hair. "Pa, how was it living with them? Ouch! Mama, softer."

His hands rub his beard, shaking loose a breadcrumb. "I'd trade it any other day just to hold my brother once more, if only for a short time. Work on a cotton plantation or rice, long as we ain't apart."

"Mama, when Ina grows up, I'll take care of her. I'll do her hair." When I tilt my head up, I see the darkness of her nose. She just nods like usual. My lap is wet with drool. My skin jumps when the saliva seeps through my clothing.

In the early morning, I wake up from a knock on the door. My left arm is over my eyes to shade the sun.

"Pardon me, girl. Can I trouble you for a glass of water? My horses and I are parched. Also, another for my friend here," a soft voice says to me.

Two elderly white men stand on the stoop, dressed impressively. The man standing on my right has dark hair. The one on my left is bald, his head shining like the moon. The one that spoke has a scruffy tone and has wrinkles on his face.

I grab a glass and fill it. I brush off a green bowl big enough for his horses.

"Much obliged, Miss," the younger but stronger man says and leaves.

The other one then introduces himself. "Well, how you doing on this fine morning? My name is Braxton."

"Sir, can I help you with anything else?" I ask.

"Yes, sorry. May I speak to one of your parents for directions out of town?" he says, friendly like.

I'll go get Pa.

I walk to their bedroom right past the wash area and wake up Pa. I shake his elbow and whisper, "Pa. Some old white man here? I gave him water but now he wants to talk about something."

He sits up. Mama rolls on her side, folding the blanket in front of her face. I see her scars on her back, shoulders, and feet. Her feet a freedom race. Then she unknowingly conceals them. Pa gets up groaning. Ina is in the middle. My sister cried all night, but now she's content with sleep.

"Well hello, son!" the well-dressed man says as Pa enters the room.

Pa is barely awake, his shirt coming down over his face. When he sees the white man, his expression spikes with disgust. The stranger is standing inside, he didn't wait for me to return with Pa.

Papa grabs me and pulls me back to his side.

"Please have a seat, my boy. Is that any way to greet your old man?"

Pa tightens his grip on me and stares at the man in stony silence.

"How old are you now, son? Flint's twenty-eight, so you are at least, what, thirty-nine? I remember the day the wife bought you. Trying to pass you off as an offspring. The flies that hovered above your head, boy, you reeked like my shits. Glad I took good care of you." He belches out an awful laugh. His heavy stomach rolls.

"The way your hand stuck out, begging for more food. Did you think you had some type of privilege over the other darkies?"

The other man steps back into the house. His expression pure cold and of someone who knew what is to come, experience bream. "I thought she wasted my hard-earned coins purchasing a dead negro."

I look back to the first man. "Well, I only came for business, son. The market is demanding more um, how can I say this delicately, workers." His grin is rich. The bags underneath his eyes are ocean waves.

I just stare at him, wondering what he is talking about.

Braxton sits down with a cane between his legs, glaring around the place. His head rotates to the table, candles, and then to his partner. "I see you made yourself a home. Flint told me a lot," he says.

Pa lets go of my wrist and lunges at Braxton, pulling him to his feet. "Out!" Pa screams.

"Pa, who is he? What's going to happen?"

Pa's face burns with anger, no more like despair. "This man's a nightmare, Abel. He is Margo's husband and a slave trader."

Braxton slaps Pa's arms off him, then fixes his own collar and tie.

Braxton pushes Pa back and taps on his hip. "Now that I have your undivided attention, let's get down to it. I'm on a tight schedule—auction's any day now."

His friend steps closer, the sound of his boots singing against the floor.

Braxton turns around and says, "Give me some time. I'm talking to my son and his daughter. What an awful act my wife committed. You were never meant to taste freedom. It took me years to find you but Flint contacted me. She gave you the long-lasting mirage of a free man. Don't you agree? And for that, I am sorry for her and myself."

"To tell you the truth, I told her to go out and buy some more slaves. Why she chose you is beyond my comprehension. I decided I would raise you to make you feel somewhat wanted, then when you were grown, sell you. Cannot trade a dying mule, now can we?"

I could tell he wanted to grin but he waited patiently for Pa reaction.

The sound of Ina crying drifts in from the next room. Neither stranger winces at the distraction.

"Well you see, here I am now," the smiling man looks at me, "I've told you once before that you were my chest and whatever treasures you came to get through your life is mine as well, remember Mootanah? There are many ways to interpret that, yet, in your case only one."

The younger man steps up. "This is not how I like to handle things. You begged me to come here now let me do what I do best! If it was your way you probably would just shoot them."

Braxton puts up his hands. I notice a silver ring on his pinky and a gold one on his pointer finger. "I'm almost done. The floor will be all yours any second. Even I find your methods repulsive. After all these years working together, you'd think my appetite to stomach your work would be stronger." Braxton laughs again. "You're a foul man," Braxton says, looking at his partner.

Mama enters, Ina cradled against her chest like a crescent moon. Her face is creased in a question. What is all this ruckus?

"Abel, go to Mama," Pa says.

Braxton speaks. "Oh, the family's assembled, I presume. My colleague is an impatient man, as you can tell."

"Good morning all." He tips his gray, narrow brim hat. His boots still clack like coins dropping on wood. "Most white men wave their guns or whips to instill fear to folks as yourselves but me, I am fear!" He walks slowly, taking off his coat and folding it on his arm like a towel. He has on black overalls. The man sparks a cigar, takes a long inhale, then smoke rush through his nose.

"What do you want?" Papa asks nervously.

"Braxton can you wait outside." He turns to Pa, timed his words, just to see Pa eyes flick dimly. "I want to give you people hell." He walks over to a pole with wooden arms coming from it and drops his jacket onto it. "Today you will lose your daughter, but more importantly yourself. We will fight one another, only way I know that will break you."

Just before the unknown stranger makes his move, he looks at me, Ina, and Mama and says, "William was one smart cracka. A physical and psychological breakdown is genius. You see here boy, when a nigger woman observes the dominant male beaten down for what he stands for, it muddles with her." He looks up at us. His body is covered with bumps and scrapes. He has dark hair and black eyes. "This is a lesson for the family. I'll only teach this once."

"If I should make you give into me, I've already won. Your daughter will think to herself if what I'm about to say will come true. Knowing this, it's a gateway to feeling attached to you. I wonder which one of the three will have it the hardest?" He looks at Ina. "Well, I guess four. I've destroyed many negroes lives, but I can't say this will be my last. It's always been my humble pleasure to tame y'all folks. Wild as a horse but useful after properly broken down and trained. You agree?" He grins, then he squats down and stretches his legs then arms. He looks comfortable while performing his art.

"If I beat your Pa, he'll no longer be able to recognize himself, realizing he couldn't save the family he loves by the same hands that built him! He'll always wonder what he did wrong, but he knows it'll haunt him.

"Now you see, your Ma here, she's the queen: a beautiful slender woman. Will she ever be able to look at him again? Will she hold resentment in her eyes or compassion? Your Ma will be the wrath of your father. Every time they talk . . . he'll be infected by hateful truths eating at him, gradually harvesting his soul. Will your love decay like a descending shadow? I'm quite curious.

"They'll grow apart without you in their presence. They'll embody shame, guilt, and most importantly, no closure. Now, if I'm right, one of you won't live for long. So, being the kind gentleman, I've brought a gift." He points at a long extended rope, coiled like a snake. William Lynch that was one smart fellow.

The stranger flexes his palms, squeezing and releasing. He smiles at Papa as if to say he is ready. He hits Papa twice on his nose and blood rushes out. Pa cocks his head, leaving the stranger with a bruise. Then they shove into one another. The stranger gets Pa off and spits out blood. They toss around everywhere together and fresh firewood rolls across the floor. They grunt and moan, Papa more so. Papa holds his breath. Both men rest, but the stranger does not seem exhausted.

"Come here boy, we aren't through." His fingers taunt Papa. Mama is still holding onto Ina, and I am worried while standing behind her.

Papa begins the next attack, his brown trouser is ripped even more. Ma covers Ina's eyes and attempts to cover both her ears too. But she is exposed to the chaos. I pray Papa stays strong. Mama's face is engrossed in wrinkles. Her mouth and eyes are open wide. My body jumps when I see Pa underneath his boots.

My fear quenches when Papa gets up. They both catch their breaths, beads of sweat rolling. There is blood on the man's shirt and Papa's right cheek. Their knuckles are torn, exposing flesh. Pa lands a strong punch on his side but the stranger does not go down but only retaliates harder. Pa starts to huff and puff, but his strength does not wave. The stranger grabs Pa's face then drives his fingers into Pa's eyes.

A strong kick to the stomach takes Pa's breath.

The taste of fear swells in my throat. The smell of blood smears my judgment. He is winning and his words approach me. I jump in after Pa. I land a good kick but smack down to the floor in pain. I hear Ina and Ma shrieking but Pa is in pain. I feel like I am about to vomit. Ma rushes over next to me. Her warm hands touch my cheeks.

I'm lying on the floor, she keeps trying to get my attention. Mama is crying and crying. All I can think about is hiding all four of us away in the small hidden space away from this madness. Both Ma's and Pa's faces are painted in my head. Ma is terrified, and as for Pa, I don't even know a word that can describe him.

Pa is crawling towards us. The unknown figure grabs his jacket and puts it back on.

"You see, boy," the man says, "Lynch came up with this appalling idea, but it makes sense. Here's another cheap lesson. The word that scares all African-American. The same word derived from him. Lynch." He squats where mama, Ina, and myself are laid, my head resting on Mama's lap.

"My prediction is you, boy, you won't survive. Make sure you use that tree out back, you hear! Look in your daughter's eyes cause it's the last time you'll ever see her." He pauses before speaking again. "Then again, this baby looks like it was only just born. How long have you had the pleasure to hold your child, ma'am? Weeks? A month? You'll see them both ripped from your clutches. Maybe the child will have it the hardest, always wondering what happened to her parents. Will you tell her this awful truth or will you lie? Abel right? Well anyways, I best be off. You folks should try to enjoy the morning. It's nice today." He hollers for Braxton and his voice echoes around the house.

Braxton walks back inside and snatches Ina then he hauls me up.

The stranger tosses me over his shoulder and I see Ma and Pa's expressions.

I scream and kick my feet. "Mama! Papa!"

Mama jumps up and claws the stranger carrying me. I have never seen her so savage-like. Her neck is thick and her eyes red. "Madam, we came to an understanding."

"Mama." Her eyes jolt at me and she continues attacking him. Braxton shoots his gun on the floor. "Keep it up and I won't miss again." She keeps going without any fear until the gun is pointed at my sister. She freezes, I freeze, then Mama drops to the floor. While Pa bleeds our names, Ma can't even yell for us.

My tale is not one I wanted to tell, but several years after my captivity and freedom I wrote Rooks of the Raven. But before I continue, there is something you need to know about my family. The choices I made in captivity felt like they were not of my own accord . . .

# Chapter 1

My name is Abel. I live in a beat up barn on the outskirts of a town called Welton. I have always dreamed of being a writer.

I have a desire to help my family and possibly, one day, move to the northern states. Maybe I will go to New York. Nobody will stop me from progressing forward there. I will save my parents from the disorder of Missouri and the immorality of the tainted souls. They deserve a fresh start, especially Mama.

Ms. Bell freed us. Margo Bell. She enjoys our company and prays that life will be different.

I believe her.

She is an angel in disguise and has never pulled any devious schemes. I suppose we live in a tasteless world. I often seek a lifestyle that's not glamorous, but more stable, hating the feeling of wondering where my next meal will come from or worse, if I will always be around my family. These are not thoughts that should buzz in my head.

My parents are forever grateful to Miss Bell. I never understood why she helps us. But why should I question it? It's better than possibly living on the streets or much worse. I dare not think about it.

Mama and Papa are outside working in our garden as I continue my lessons in her lovely home. I yearn for what she has—literacy.

"Here child, let us continue with your teachings. How much do you remember?"

I give her a blank face.

"You don't remember anything, do ya, Abel?"

My face sours. "No, sorry. I try, I really do. It's just I can't remember much. It's hard!"

She raises my head high up, her pointer finger under my chin and says, "Abel deary, don't give up. I know it's hard, but eventually, you will get it. Trust me. And you know what else?"

"What?" I ask.

"You could teach others. Wouldn't that be funny?"

She sat down with me for hours until I became comfortable. I detest letters that are silent. My counting skills are awful but I can read dates fairly easy. It's like January, February, March, and Saturday and then on—just teasing . . . I know what goes next.

Margo's hair is short and always curly. Her spectacles compliment her eyes, light blue as calm wind.

"Bell? How come there are a hundred ways to describe the same one word, like good, great, or even excellent? It's stupid if you ask me."

"I'm not sure, dear. But once you find out, I'll be the first to listen." Her wrinkles spring alive when she grins.

"Thanks for practice." I hug her and exit. Papa always told me never to overstay my welcome. Don't become a trouble-some girl, he says.

I race into the barn, more ecstatic than I have ever been.

"Slow down, Abel. Why you in such a hurry?" Pa asks ea-gerly. He looks like he was thinking as he rises from the bed. The scent of tomatoes is on his body.

I brush some grass off his shoulders.

We have one bed that all three of us share. It's a tight squeeze but it's something we don't mind. Knowing I can twist to my left and see Mama or to my right to snuggle with Pa, even bitter cold days can warm up.

I scream. "Look, I can finally spell my name. See." I hear Mama applaud while she is folding clothes.

Mama's face swells with grief. I can tell each day hurts. She has a small cut on her left ear with bumps and scrapes on her face. Ma's eyes state so much that she never speaks aloud.

I show them my worn out bundles of papers. I flip through until I found a clean sheet. In big print, I spell, "A-B-L-E." I retire the night away, sound asleep. Tomorrow is church.

Church is like listening to the ocean, just in a different lan-guage. We go often. The color of the church is bland. The building looks like children came together and crafted it. They told me the Lord doesn't care about how it is built; he looks past that and sees the people inside, loving us all. The wood looks crisp from the aftermath of a fire.

I'm pleased knowing they are willing to take us in despite our appearances and clothing. Usually, I have kinks in my hair, as brushing it hurts terribly. Arriving, I greet my two friends. Even though Pa is not the pastor, he is kind of important. Papa has faith in his words and can raise everyone's spirits.

"Hi Abel!" Aya walks up to me. She's a friend that I only see at church.

"Hey, Aya. Sit next to me."

She squeezes me like a snake then gives me a kiss on the cheek, one on each side. Her blue bow brushes my cheek. I'm not sure why we do that but I guess it's from watching the grown folks.

They look silly, like one peck isn't good enough.

"Not today, Abel. I'm sitting with Cleo. Join us will ya?" Aya has high socks and a small faded purple skirt. I look at Ma, and she nods her head, pushing my upper back in the direction Aya is moving.

Songs play, though I'm not sure what instrument they are using. People are up and singing, an amazing morning as usual. I have so much faith because of Papa.

"God is good."

"Amen."

I see black, white, and blue blouses on women. Most of the women wear hats as wide as doors. Their lips are like roses and darken at the top. Most gentlemen have low-trim hats. Faces are clean and they wear black suits. Both males and females sport dark slick shoes. My family and a few others are looking poor. Even Aya smells clean.

After church, I usually venture to Welton Town, trying to sell corn or anything from the garden. Most people look at me in disgust. Despite my outcome, I always try. I beg in fact, hoping they will buy anything from me. Coming home emp-ty-handed is frustrating.

There are several shops around. The ground is covered with dirt and gravel. They say it's a family place, but ironically fail to mention which families are permitted.

My feet hurt from the sharp pebbles. My basket dances around my arm and I'm careful not to drop it. I have sweet corn, fresh cucumbers, spicy peppers, carrots, and this purple plant.

I walk past small restaurants teeming with laughter, but only from faces opposite from my own.

"Pardon me, Ma'am, would you—" She doesn't bother to look at me. But the way her head jerks tells me all I need to know. She picks up her speed.

The town square is filled with stores ranging from clothing, toys, and shoe repair shops and taverns. They favor taverns the most. I see two men getting their shoes shined. "Morning. I have cucumbers, carrots, pepper and—"

"Pepper and your eggplant please." It's apparently called an eggplant. I have to try and remember.

His rough hands shake my basket looking for more options.

"Pardon me, brother. In a hurry," the other black man says. The worker reminds me of an ant, always working. Coins clink as he reaches in his pocket.

"Thank you," I say and skip off.

After going around, I have enough coins for sugar, milk, and flour. Across from the shoe shiner, I buy my supplies. I wave my empty basket at him. A different guy taps him on his shoulder for attention. His new cloth waves like a white flag.

I always see kids running out of stores, excited about a new toy that their Ma or Pa just bought. Those children are lucky. At least my basket is filled with new food, except for one purple plant. I bite into it. My tongue curls in disgust. I immediately spit out the seeds.

Welton School ranges from the first year to eighth grade. They are strict on who is welcome to pass their gates. The town is divided by a railroad track that flows through its center. New faces walk around looking for a steady place to call home. The ravens hover about, loud with their calls.

The town is not big. For income, they allow blacks to live among them without too many racial issues, or that's what I believe.

I hurry home. Papa in his same torn trouser and brown shirt.

"Margo has a surprise for you, go see her," he says, the lantern flickering in the background; it hangs on a nail swinging ever so slightly. I leave the basket on the bed. "Have Mama make us bread when she gets back fetching water."

# Chapter 2

Margo's home is nice. She has a fireplace that illuminates her entire living space. Two chairs are simply placed alongside each other. Her sofa casts a shadow that engulfs her small bookshelf.

"Abel." I smile when I hear her voice. She turns around and places a pan on her damaged table. The table has marks that stretch far but have no direction or purpose, almost as if someone deeply dug their nails into it.

"Hello Ms. Bell. How are you?" I say. A sweet smell covers the room.

Now that I think about it, her house is small. She uses her table to cook and eat. On top of her broken sewing stand are some pins.

In her drawers are her pen and papers ready to torture me with more spelling. The lower drawer has a deep, rounded bottom for her threads. I'm grateful for her sewing craftsmanship. She made Mama a dress.

"I'm fine, deary." She chokes on her words, then clears her itchy throat. "Ready for more practice?"

I nod my head in agreement, as she hands me freshly-made treats.

Her necklace dangles as she hunches over. The food tingles in my mouth with a cozy touch and melts on my tongue. It's the type of taste that makes you sing and dance as others look at you crazy like.

We sit down. Her gown is narrow at the hips; she is wearing pear-shaped earrings and gloves with white brogan shoes. It's all so fine compared to my sewn outfit made from sacks; she is stunning.

Bell teaches me many more concepts such as time, dates, and more reading and writing. I am finally absorbing her teaching. However, I still need practice, a lot more.

"Okay, let's practice on those silent letters. Spell writer."

I stare at a blank wall. Her kitchen entrance has a see-through cloth nailed to the wood. I can see my favorite sitting spot outside.

"Stop that," she demands.

"Stop?" I say.

Her gloved hands are on my knees. I guess I was tapping my foot again.

I spell it for her, righter. The ink drips on one spot, making a small pool due to thinking too hard.

She blurts with a kind laugh, "You really don't like silent letters." Then she shows me.

Bell glances at me.

"Abel, don't stare. Use your words; articulate." She huffs at her glasses. The hotness of her breath clouds the lenses. Margo uses her gown and cleans them.

"Can we read one of your books?" I ask. We head to her bedroom and she begins to read. I laugh at her. "You sound like a man, Ms. Bell."

She always tells me I have to get into character and become the character. When she does it, it just looks silly.

I follow her finger along the thinly laid pages with huge dark letters. My head falls on her soft shoulder.

"Okay," she says. "Let's finish this later and return to the table."

An aggressive knock on her door diverts our attention. She slowly picks herself up, hands on her knees as she pushes off. I hear small cracks from her bones with each step followed by short exerted grunts.

She slowly picks herself up, hands on her knees as she pushes off. I hear small cracks from her bones with each step followed by short exerted grunts.

"Who can that be?" she murmurs. "Flint?" Her voice juggles with both relief and worry.

Flint is Ms. Bell's only child and she loves him more than anything. But he hates us. A long time ago, Flint pushed me. He hates the fact that I was becoming educated, possibly exceeding him. Ms. Bell is the only person who can keep the beast in its cage.

I stand up slowly, keeping the chair from squeaking. I slide over to a hiding spot for situations like this. It's behind the large sewing stand. If needed, the floorboard lifts up and we can hide underneath. The stand is pushed up far enough without me moving it. I patiently wait and peep through a small hole. The hole is not easily noticed.

"Mother, are they in here?" he says, standing by the table.

"No honey, I'm alone. And good to see you as well." She gives him what looks like a kiss on the cheek, and her arm disappears into a hug.

"I heard you talking. Who were you talking to?" For my sake, I'm glad there is no door knob.

"Are you drinking again? You've been gone for all these years and this how you present yourself, like your father?" A glass shatters. I hear pieces scattering like mouse footsteps.

"Mother! Don't lie to me and don't you disrespect Father. What he does is necessary! Why are there two glasses on the table? Are you helping her again? Mother, look at me. Are you helping her again?"

Bell bends to pick up the shattered piece. I hear her grunts. The only two times she moans is to get up or bend over.

"Are you out of work again? Is that why you are back home? Or did your father not want to see you? I told you to stay away from him. What he does is awful. Why do you think I left?"

"Don't get attached. Remember who they are?" Flint says. It's quiet. The space I'm in is cramped and dark. If I'm quiet maybe I can sneak through the front.

They continue arguing. I'm so scared if I were to get caught I wouldn't know what to do. Flint began to search his home, as if he had lost his keys or wallet. A home he hadn't been in for some time.

"Flint something downstairs I want you to see," Margo says. The door shuts. I tip toe once their voices disappear.

Outside, the darkness is winning. I'm not sure how long I've been hiding.

Out of breath, I try to muster what might be words. "Ma . . . Mama . . . Pa . . . Fli . ..." My breath catches up. "Flint! He is back!" I yell and I see Pa begin to freeze up.

The last time Flint saw him, it wasn't pleasant.

Ma's hands squeezes Pa's and my own giving off a comfortable feeling like she does. For the rest of the night we assume he would barge in and cause a ruckus.

Ma blew out the candles.

A new day presents itself as Pa and I work in the garden attending to small tasks. I wear my sack sewn dress me and Mama share. I think she made it with potato sacks; the dress is a thick black fabric.

The door flutters as Flint steps through. His almond shaped head ignites his rough prickly hair brighter than fire. His cuffs push to his elbow with white shirt underneath. Flint has brown trouser and suspenders. Nasty brown boots, like he jogged in mud. He is a drunk. His plan is to make our life miserable. He's a mosquito that won't let up, draining and wearing us down.

Flint laid his grubby hands on his mother real bad once. I remember her sitting on the porch steps arguing. Papa grew tired of his rude behaviors and pushed him off. Pa and Ms. Bell have a history together that I don't know much about. He never tells me much of his past. All I know is he once was a slave. His back held proof, strong with thick veins.

The second he steps out he starts harassing Pa. "Hey old man, can you spell too?" He continues, "I haven't forgotten about my promise. So here's what we gonna do." He spits on the gravel, his spit hung from his mouth. Takes one last bite of a fuzzy apple, I think he ate the stem. His elbows like powder. "If you beg for forgiveness, I might just do that. How does that sound?" Flint laughs stumbling inside.

I sneak in literature lessons when Flint roves his way to town. But it doesn't really feel the same. I have observed through the years when her son is around, sometimes she forgets to keep her disguise, the kind woman. She acts like she forgot her role.

Today is scorching hot as we immerse ourselves in work. I help mama with washing.

She does not have many talents, but I adore Mama. My younger sibling resides in Ma's belly. We try not to have her work, hopefully preventing any illness. However, it will be difficult having a baby around. I'll try to help out as best I can. We don't have much of anything, including clothes—three maybe four sets of shirts and dresses.

Mama looks at me intensely. "What? Why are you in front of me?"

I pull her aside. Papa and Flint are at each other's throats. I look at Ma, then back. "Where is Ms. Bell?" She shakes her head. "What should we do?" To jump in would be jumping into a river to save someone knowing I cannot swim as well.

Flint is now shouting loudly. Papa stands there, not moving nor flinching, a complete statue. "What's the matter, Moot? Can't you see that I'm talking to you!" He kicks over Papa's bucket. Why is he doing so much to inflict woe?

Papa opens his mouth and speaks with tenderness, but a subtle rage sparks. "Why are you so miserable? What do you want? Maybe the shirt off my back, or maybe shoes that I don't have. Is that it?" He bends over and collects the corn, piece by piece.

Flint retaliates, unfortunately not with his words. He beats Papa. Ma starts to sob, without realizing her hands are firmly gripped on her belly.

I guess Flint is exhausted because he stops? Several minutes later, Ms. Bell finally shows up, strolling in her wagon. I spot her from afar but do not want to believe such awful thoughts. She steps out and pats her horses. They neigh as she feeds them small sugar cubes.

Sadness and guilt surround Margo. Did she just watch? Papa struggles over, placing his weight on his right leg. "Abel, don't worry. I'm fine." He smiles like nothing happened. His tan trouser is smothered with dirt.

"Pa!" He walks past me as if I am invisible. His eyes are like two bronze pennies, glossy with grief. The birds above screech as if someone plucked a feather.

Night approaches and we withdraw into our home. I lie in the dark of the night, lost in my thoughts. Everything I once believed betrays me. I'm engulfed in anger but mostly sadness. I stand and go over to a bench that sits in disarray from every-thing. It holds no meaning in the world, but it was there. Just like how I feel at times. It's pointed away from the farm and in the distance. The bench has two arms that hold your lower back and has a nighttime dark color. My head swivels as the kitchen candles blow out behind me. Her home is dark like the night.

I lift my leg up and bury my face.

# Chapter 3

Walking into town is a daunting experience. Though I don't walk in their stores, I like to look at the fancy shoes. I view from the window, mesmerized by every color, and the designs of clothes or toys until I hear, "shoo girl! Go away. Bother someone else."

I go to the bench for a quiet place to sit and relax but did not realize I am in enemy territory. A few kids approach me.

"What are you doing here?" says the tubby kid, standing in front of his pack. His top lip is like a toad wart. "Can't you read?"

I ignored his last word. I swallow, then try to reason with the other children. "Sorry, I don't know how to read," I say timidly, as I stand up and use a safety pin to keep my papers together. Pebbles and gravel have grass creeping through the crevice.

A kid says, "It's just like them; they are all useless," one of the last boys adds with a laugh, "Yeah, I hate them."

"Lies, shut up!" A girl steps up. "Move over Tommy. It says whites only." She points intensely at a blurry object. She is lying. It says no such thing. "Now you know. Besides this area is too nice for people like you." She sounds like she is thirty years old, chewing on a piece of paper. I hear two of them say, "Stick it on her."

I knock her hand away, dropping the sticky damp paper on the ground. Now I'm being chased by a pack of hunters.

Confused and fearful. I'm being chase because I touched her? No, that's not it. Maybe that paper was her favorite meal, I might be angry as well if I were in her place. Then again, that cannot be right. The girl's red blouse is in the far back. I hear the sound of metal, maybe coins or shoe buckles.

They are gaining on me. My heart is racing with unwanted excitement, beating faster than I can run. Left then a right turn. Under the swings? I kick dirt at them. It hurts my feet; small rocks dig into my skin.

"Leave me alone!" My chest pounds like a drum circle.

They start throwing rocks at me. So I kept on running. I take a turn but there were no exit wound. They creep at me slowly and menacingly.

"We have her now!" they tease, booming with laughter with each darkening step. I continue to think, what should I do?

"What should we do?" Tommy asks as he catches up to everyone. "Make her respect her Kings." His round face jiggles as he grins.

They start pounding me as Flint did to my Pa. They did not stop. They have an intense bloodlust to maim me, and I'm panicking. My head is hurting, my body is sore, and my heart is shatter, bleeding with poison.

I curl into a strong rock, one hand on my papers the other covering my face. The feel of their shoestrings on my leg.

"What is this, a potato sack?" Their voices flare.

I start to think, plotting my next move. I had to make it count. I wait for an opening then . . . yes, I'm free. Somehow, I gain strength. I feel lighter, my legs feel like I'm carrying two Tommy's, on my back. I am fading with fatigue.

"Ouch!" I screech. There is no way out. My hair is pulled back and I hit the ground again. Hi ground, lovely day, think I might have to live with you if that's okay.

I faintly hear a bark. All I know is a knight saved me. A small dog appeared, it looks as if it leaped in paint. Its stomach white and on top white and black splotch fight for territory.

Though it is small, it had an unbeatable attitude and rescues me by scaring off those cruel kids. The group of kids runs away, laughing and high-fiving each other. The girl in red says, "I hope daddy will be happy. I did exactly what he said." She is proud, her first hunt.

I look up. My vision is still blurry. My tongue rubs against my teeth. To my surprise, none are missing.

"Hey, can you hear me? Are you okay?" The dog speaks?

"Who are you, what are you?" I hear myself whispering.

As I focus, I see a boy about my age, but definitely taller. He has an indent on the side of his cheek, making him all the more charming. He has soft brown eyes and hair. His face is whiter than snow but a gentle smile follows.

"Hi, I'm Corjo. Nice to meet you." He helps me stand. I notice his gray button-up shirt, with black knee breeches, and white stockings rising to his knee.

"Where do you live?" I point in a direction as he slowly carries me, my arms are around his shoulder. "What's your name?"

I hesitate before I answer his question. "I . . . I'm Abel." I rub my head.. It is hard to speak as the blood in my mouth makes it feel like I'm eating a lump of porridge. I then stare at his dog. Corjo, he smells nice.

"That's Milo. He is very friendly, despite what you saw—a softy always willing to protect." The dog starts to sniff me then anxiously waits for me as his tail swings back and forth. We stop.

"What does he want? Is he trying to eat me? Its tasting me now."

He chuckles. "He likes you. He wants you to shake. Look, like this." A sharp pain hits me as he lets me go. Pain shoots to my right knee.

He starts to pet and shake his dog's paw. "Did you want to pet him?" He rises to his feet, then scans me. With a sympathetic look he says "They took your shoes? I am terribly sorry."

"They didn't take my shoes," I respond.

He looks puzzled for a moment. "Oh, then they'll be around here somewhere. You look over here and I'll search over there. Milo, you help as well, sniff out the scent of a summer breeze."

I stop him by his arm muscle. "No! that's not what I meant!"

"Okay?"

I stare at the ground, not wanting to tell him. I did not want him to laugh at me.

"I see, you never had shoes to begin with." His next move is something I could not have believed if I didn't witness it. He takes his shoes off and hurls them at a building. "Now we are the same. We are equals and will always be that way." He sticks his pinky out.

"What you doing?"

He grins. "It's a pinky swear. It could mean a lot of things but mainly it keep your promises and it's another sign for the absolute truth, at least for me it is."

I wish he hadn't said that because I instantly snap back to knowing that equal is a made up word. I shout as if my head will burst, "Equal? You think we are equals?" I begin to wonder if this boy is helping me or if he is planning something? Uncertain, I flail my arms until free. I run and run until his presence is no more, a whisper in the wind. My body feels heavy but the pain stops throbbing. He does not chase me but instead crouches down to his dog.

I approach Bell's farm. You can always tell it by the red fence. It runs all the way from Margo's house, to the shed, then stops at the bottom of a small hill near the creek. The other side is an open field with my bench. Though small, the garden divides both homes in the center. A shovel and a rake lean against each other like old friends. Those same tools have been here for a long time, chunky with rust.

A figure that means little to me stands by her door. "Hello, Abel!" She sounds ill. I ignore her gesture and run towards the barn. Ma and Papa are not in sight. "Abel deary, what's the matter?" The air muffles her voice. I finally stop and glare at. Her hands clutch the blue rails. I almost run over to her but flashbacks come flooding in. "Don't you want more lessons?"

"No Ma'am! I don't want lessons from you any longer."

"Abel? Please talk to me. You love when I teach or read to you!" Her hand jumps across her heart. Her voice quivers. Her words feel so real. I release an irritated smirk, did something happen?

As I walk away, I add, out of pure boldness. "I saw you the other day as my dad was brutally attacked. Why?"

She does not say anything, but guilt floods her face. She coughs into a plaid handkerchief. Her cough grows violently louder. Her nose is red like the veins on her arms. I hope my anger passes soon but it's not the first time she's played dirty. I try not to say her name, as I just call her she from then on.

I bury my feelings when I see my folks.

"How was town?" Papa asks. I hide my face in the sheets of paper. "Oh, it was fun. I met a boy."

Mama looks back at me, cutting bread. The knife sounds like a door knock. "That's interesting. What's his name?" I stutter trying to remember is name. "C-C-Corjo, I think that what he said."

Pa asks how my lessons are going. I told him everything is going well, still covering my face. I look both my parents in the eyes and lies, which I don't do ever. He doesn't ask me more questions.

Nothing makes sense any longer. I need something to ground me back to how I was, the young and naïve girl, Abel D. Bloom. Like her table—no direction.

I humbly prayed that day, to whom, I don't even know. I swore my allegiance to one God, but could not comprehend why.

# Chapter 4

1858

Every winter our shed decays slowly. The cold breeze seeps in. We struggle for warmth. My nose hurts when I breathe and my toes are layered with warm cloths. I hate it. I look even more stupid. Work becomes simpler as our life had lost its structure. We can't harvest any crops but keep some food for desperate days.

We walk past the red fence. The morning air is cool but restless. During the cold season, we do not attend church as much. I can barely see the church beyond the Welton school. Men and women dress warmly, with plaid and plain scarves with heavy coats like ourselves.

"Abel what's wrong?" Pa asks. I'm in between them. Behind us our footprints allure me. We pass by the window of Dave's Dresses. I see a gown, glistening white. Blue gloves plaster through the window. Mama paused for a second staring too. Her hands squeezes my left palm. More people walk past. Top hats white with snow, they sneeze and cough. "Mama you okay." Pa and myself several feet ahead of her.

Mama stumbles into a stranger, making her lose her balance, though she does not fall, nor does he. "Our apologizes, Sir," Pa says.

The gentleman sneers. His woman attaches to his elbow. She wears red gloves reaching to her elbow. "How rude," she says. "Can she not speak for herself?" A wagon passes by.

More people crowd around. Their eyes more vicious than their speech. Few woman wrap in dark fur. White bonnet hats. Most in red or white wool cape and dark leather boots. Men in plaid trouser and jeans heavy dark boots and coats. Some fancy with gold watch.

"What was that?" the crowd says. My ears ring. Horses and wagons stop as the drivers are looking past the tall white and red brick school. My hand jerked from Pa tugging me. "Abel, move." The crowd starts arguing, stun at the distance blast. The loud commotion helped us get home but we never made it to church.

Days later we find out that the church collapsed.

Later that month.

I decide to go check the church. One side droops with piles of wood. The stained glass window is shattered into pieces of red, green, and white ornaments.

I stumble into Corjo on my way back home. My face is wet with tears. I see his dog jumping and biting as Corjo throws snow. The tree beside them is dead with zero leaves. The pebbles beneath my feet are softer than before. Corjo is layered in a thick red coat and gray wool trousers. Milo is wearing a red scarf.

"It's you," he says after Milo barks. The dog's tongue is pink and wet. Our breath sprays like powder. To my surprise, his feet like my own are wrapped in bed sheets. "Would you like to come over?" The words curl back into my throat.

His head cocks like his dog's. "Yes," he say finally after pausing for so long. "I like the color of your dress. Red is my favorite color."

We talk as I lead him back home.

"Abel, who's your friend?"

Corjo interrupts, "Corjo D. Jones, Sir, nice to meet you."

"Call me Moot," Pa says.

"I did not get your name Ma'am," Corjo says. Mama looking at me. She thick with a white cape around her torso. I draw Corjo attention from Ma to my scarps of papers.

"Hey look our middle name the same letter," I say. Corjo and I are the only two cross legged on the floor.

He apologizes to Mama, his nose shows a hint of red. "Sorry come again," I cut in. "I'm Abel D. Bloom." He looks at me.

"What does the C stand for in your name?" Corjo ask. Pointing at the letter D.

"It's a 'D.'"

"That's what I meant, just like me. What does your stand for?"

"Not telling, what yours?" I ask.

"Then I'm not saying anything either." He is laughing but serious.

He did not know how to spell or read? Whichever makes more sense. The white fabric boarding the window flutters. The melting snow trickles through our heavy oak door.

We huddle on the ground. A small desk to set our bowls on. The soup strong with ginger. It's cold but the bread warms the belly. We use four metal cups with rust on its exterior and spoons.

"So you can't read either?" I say. Corjo to the left of me.

Ma quietly eats but her ears are alive. "Pa come sit," I say. He's over by the big tin can that flip down, on top a soft blanket. The tin for bathing but since its cold we brought it inside. There are dead flower petals spread for scent. At times I wonder if anybody is expose to a harder life.

We bathe maybe three days apart. All three carrying a pale bucket from the creek. The creek like a market because we get everything from there. Pick flower petals and spread in the large tin can during bath. Pa bathes first then Mama and me share.

"Corjo do you?" I ask.

"No, I never learned. Can you?"

"Only a bit. But I can teach you, it's the least I can do." We ate our meal in silence. I'll admit it, it's different having someone like him around. "This is delicious." In the midst of silence, he manages to bring up small laughs. I can tell Papa wanted to ask questions.

During the weeks I teach him lessons in the shed. He caught up to speed, sharp as a pin.

"What's next?" he asks with haste. "That's all I know if you can find a book or newspaper we can learn more together." He went home past noon that day.

I patiently sat on my bench and surrounded myself with the soothing sounds of the wind waiting for Corjo. three ravens perch on Margo roof squawking. The idea about that awful day the town tried to gang up on my Papa and how the kids attacked me. It loops back into my memory. Mama didn't mean to bump into that man; it's not her fault she couldn't apologize.

I teach Corjo lessons in the shed. He catches up quickly; he is sharp as a pin. "What's next?" He asks with haste and determination. "That's all I know. If you can find a book or newspaper, we can learn together." He went home past noon.

I wait patiently on my bench and surrounded myself with the soothing sounds of the wind and three ravens perched on Margo's roof. I think about that awful day they beat on my Papa and how the kids attacked me. Mama didn't mean to bump into that man; it's not her fault she couldn't apologize.

Days come and go but he never came. Snow is hard on the ground. Unfortunately, I'm still not talking to her.

She says, "Please, deary. Forgive me." I scurry off, faster than the rats that often steal our food. She had recently started tearing up when I did that. I became cold like her. I almost did give into her but stood strong. I wish I could forgive but I could not this time.

Corjo finally shows. "I'm here. Guess what, I brought a chess board and its kin, it's manual. He says excitedly. "Kin also means related. Look, the way I see it we can play lots of games as we learn to read." He hands some papers over. "Sorry my uncle took me to his house for a small visit."

"Wouldn't it make more sense to know how to play before we you know, play?" I say. "My uncle taught me the basics. Such as pieces name and how they move But before I came back here. I met Margo she appears to be a well groom lady."

He looks down and murmurs, "A mother. Margo said to tell you she is sorry." Maybe she was and I'm being stupid. I think I will go see how she doing. Maybe she can teach us both to read and write. I do miss those nights cuddling with her while she reads.

Weeks come and go.

Corjo and I sit on the dark bench playing. I ask, "What Margo is up to."

He answers, "Actually, I don't know. I have not seen her. I usually go around the house since she knows me."

We play more chess games and do more reading.

Flint barges into our shed. His hands rub together trying to keep warm. He huffs hot air into his palms then touches his nose. "Here's a letter my mother left for you. She asked me to deliver it." He unfolds a crumpled up letter and shuffles it belligerently my way. It is stiff and cold. He then adds, "Mother is dead by the way, she was a Pawn of an illness."

"How long have you had this?" By the time I cook up the courage to ask, he is gone. The snow crunches beneath his boots like crackers. I look at Pa. He has no idea. His sigh releases slowly. A heavy blanket grips his entire body.

Corjo picks up the envelope. Ms. Bell was gone and I did not even know. I knew she was sick but . . . I knew I didn't want to see her, but not like this. Corjo rushes to Flint. "Excuse me, sir. This reads a year ago. How long has she past?"

He did not answer.

Corjo starts to unfolds the envelope. "Should I open it?"

I shake my head in disagreement as he stops.


January of 1859.

We sit down on my bench playing chess and practice with the nice weather surrounding us. We sound out words that are new and fascinating. His feet are dirty like ours.

"Your turn." He points at a random word after ruffling through the newspaper. "Spell this one."

Every time we play, it always ends with us in a stalemate. Two rooks face off, one white and the other black. Rooks stand tall, at its finest, as it always progresses. If necessary, it moves backwards but only for a purpose, to advance. No one could make a rook flip over. And if they somehow did, it's unbothered. "Another!" he shouts as the fuel of competition heats. But of course, I do not back down. My back hunches like a hill hovering over the board. I go back to the shed. "Where has Corjo run off to?"

"Home I suppose." Ma lets out a sigh. Pa looks beaten down like he has lost me or Mama. I can't help shake that she is an important piece to him.

# Chapter 5

I glance at Pa. "Please tell me more about Ms. Bell?"

"Sit down, Abel, as I tell you the story of my mistress or what I might say, my mother."

"Mother?" Ma is outside washing our clothes. Papa and I sit on the bed.

"I was a slave that she set free. Long before you or Ma came into my life. I thank Christ every day for you two. I was a young kid getting auctioned far from Missouri. She had not always lived here. I didn't know my exact whereabouts."

"They were bidding fiercely, obtaining all the sturdy gentleman and women. Each slave was bathed in oil to look more presentable. The whites didn't even see us as people. I must have been twelve. Mamas crying over their children, holding them so tight you might as well pull the baby's arms apart because Ma's were not letting their child go. Abel, it had me in tears. I'll never let that happen to you. I cannot. It's not something I wish to put you through like Ma and me. This why we live like we do.

"I was so scared for my life, like anyone would be. I remember how the slaves begged but no one listened. Fathers! Grown men weeping at the horrific sight of his family leaving, never seen again, can you imagine. It's the saddest moment I lived through. I was a boy who served no purpose, useful to no one. You should have seen me. They prepped me for sale. Like rust standing next to steel, no one wanted me.

"Still up, the bids drew to a closure. The howl of the buyers thin as they acquired their slave. The sun growing weak with light and buyers are leaving the docks losing interest. Five of us were left. I hear the man in charge, his beard and loud voice still haunts me. He wore a gray vest with high white socks and leather boots. His hair was dark like the cane he pointed with. I remember every small detail, it's not something you forget. "Anyone want this one? Boy's of fine physique, already separated from their families, broken down to the dirt. How about her, going into motherhood? Fine breeding, just look at her hips. Have you more slaves in no time."

"No one wanted me, nor the kid next to me. They bid for the attractive woman, no older than thirty. Then her offspring, but only when she begged to have all her children. 'Cooks real nice meals for ya.' The way she begged, begged until they just accepted it. She took off with two women wearing blue bonnets, their corsets tight around their chest."

"There were only two of us left. The waves of the ocean were washing in. The boat I came in was still docked, a small one at that. Flies hovered around my body. The boy to my right was in tears. The man in charge started to wave a gun around. He probably thought we would collapse in a day or two of working, or better yet slaving. He commanded us to go to our knees. I stood still till he cracked me with his cane. 'Boss, we have to go back to England,' I heard the voice of his right-hand man. I remember because he the same one who threw my mama overboard. The captain's hands were on the silver pistol. It was a day that I wish I could forget because it still terrifies me. I heard his gun cock."

Pa runs his hands over his eyes, looking like he hasn't slept in weeks. "I promised the boy everything would be fine, that there would be another day, a brighter day. Abel, I begged, and I begged till blood drew from my throat. Soon my words turned to a sorrowful belch of pleading but he wouldn't listen. 'Well boys, you wasted my hard earned money,' the captain said. 'Do you realize how much it cost going to Liberia? I lost good men.'

"The boy stared at me, kneeling on the platform eyes of the youth and innocence and tried to tell me something . . . crack! Blood flowed from that boy as if he was a sheep. Though chained, I crawled towards him. His eyes were still open but nothing spilled from his lip but blood. Another cocking sound, and my mouth went dry just waiting, waiting. I wanted to run but would not get far. My feet were chained to death's door.

"But then, Mrs. Bell yelled from the crowd, 'I want him, sir!' However rough you think her voice may be, that day it was a song of grace. She was young and beautiful, so filled with life like the world was hers. Her hair was longer but she had the same glasses. She ran to me like a cloud, her elegant puffy dress with the same necklace swimming around her neck. She also had a bracelet that sparkled gold. Her stagecoach was fancy and black.

"That day, Abel, she saved my life. So Flint and I grew up together. I looked after him on some nights, cleaned up his mess, or whatever they commanded. I lived a new and strange life.

Saddened by the loss of her child, Bell fell into depression. Her husband never forgave her nor showed an ounce of compassion. He took it out on me and the few others around the house. I forget his name now.

"I grew up with the Bells. Their home was like two houses put together. Two people slept together in small dark huts. We cultivated rice and grains. His land was small, with maybe ten slaves, all in tan rough spun cloth. Her husband was abusive towards me, but she shielded me the best she could. There were nights that I became acquainted with flogging, and often what felt like torture. I had a place of belonging and held on even if it was not the best.

"Growing up, I happened to be the only one who fought Flint since we were the two youngest. We would get into a vicious argument. Flint adored his father. Whenever we ate, I sat in the corner, plate in hand, devouring my meal with the dirtiest of fingers after a long day's work. They were at the table. On some nights, Bell would have me for supper, just the

two of us. I felt alive, like a human instead of a slave. She talked about her life. I sat quiet and ate, never asked for seconds
but somehow she knew. She walked back, stirred her pot, then
poured me more. The beef stew was splendid with peppers.

"Margo had enough and ran from her gruesome husband.
She moved to Missouri, taking me and Flint, leaving the old
man behind. She acquired this farm. Growing up in Welton
Town is where I met your Ma. She cannot speak of her past,
unable to let it out. Ma was a slave but she had a much more
abusive life, transforming her into how you know her. The
slave owner who attained your mother must have been beyond
ruthless.

"An opportunity arose and she ran for hours, possibly days,
honestly, I don't know how she ended up here, but I'm glad.
Ma came stumbling by the farm, beaten up, and her clothes
torn and tattered. Her blood was dried; she was wheezing and
coughing. I could tell what they had done to her. Her body
resembled my own but far worse. Her back appeared to have
spelled something from the crack of the whip, a repugnant
sight. I won't say but it's engraved on her body, transforming
her into what she is now—a mute.

"Ms. Bell took Mama in at my request. Days maybe a week
later, scouts came looking, Bell had hidden her in the . . . well
you know the spot. We avoided danger for the time. Welton
Town was not as big as it is now. Your Ma and I, we fell in love
thus had you a breath of fresh air."

Pa kisses me on the forehead and I take his large hands and
kiss them.

"Years passed. Stores were built and it became lively. Many come, as some fled. This town is known for its ravens. Ravens bring a mysterious and ominous feel to Welton Town. Each bird having knowledge of all events; that's what I believe, so watch for them.

"When you were small, Margo committed an awful crime that she buried; we all did. She took a life from a young boy, his mother. She was drawing unnecessary attention, but Margo had no intentions of giving you up. They would take us all and punish Bell for hiding us. We buried her underneath the bench that sits outside. Abel some secrets are best left in the dark.

"Long story short, everything she did was for you. She loved you like the daughter she had lost. The days of your youth were tough; you never gave her a chance. She wanted you to succeed, to be happy. I asked, no, we asked her to give you a better life. Why do you think you cherish books so much? New York? I bet she told you stories that made you smile. She gave you everything she stood for. She a fighter."

Papa walks away, pushes the sturdy shed doors, and goes outside. I stare at the letter, still sealed, stopping any more tears from escaping. Even if I open it, what purpose would this letter serve?

It's different living with a mute. My life is filled with challenges but this is not one of them; it never will be. Mama is a woman of no words but her actions speak for her. I try to respect her wishes and never pry too much. But a daughter with curiosity is quite persistent. I'm stubborn.

I hate the idea of what my ma went through to keep her from forever talking. I can only imagine the sorrow that seeps out of her scars day in and out.

Pa took years to figure out his lover's life with constant gestures and questions resulting in head nods. He is a devoted man, though at times it became complex. I've seen mother's back, only once by accident . . . All I know is, the Rooks still linger.

# Chapter 6

My mind soars with new knowledge. Corjo and I still have an intense hunger to learn. We also spend more time with one another, gradually becoming closer. I find myself thinking about him when he is not around, like what he's doing at the moment or is he reciprocating the same emotions.

Every time he comes, Milo accompanies him now. I grew fond of that dog as well, gentle and adorable from head to tail. He is a playful pet, but Ma and Pa jump at his presence, flinching at every bark. Flashback of their past I suppose. Dogs were used to control us savages, or my ancestors.

"Good morning everyone."

"Hey, Corjo. It's been a while since we last saw you," Pa responds.

"I've been busy trying to keep my dad out of trouble. He is a difficult man to deal with," Corjo says.

We head towards the bench. "I don't think your mother very fond of me. She never speaks to me. Did I do something wrong?"

I held in a small grin. "Mama thinks of you as a hero and don't you forget it. I told her how you helped me."

"If that's true, how come she never talks to me?"

I exhale then place my trust in him. I place my hand on his solid white shirt sleeves.

"Ma lost her voice long ago, way before I was born. She doesn't talk. We communicate differently."

Corjo gives a fascinating look, wide mouth but does not seem shocked. "So how do you know if she needs anything? Wait, don't answer I can imagine, she is your mother. There's a connection that only you guys share a bond that links you passed blood. Something ridiculous like that right?" We laugh. "She doesn't need much from us. At times she has her on little signals for communication.

A horde of ravens flocks above our heads. The sky is clear and I feel great. "So did you want to play?" I ask him.

"Of course, but I was hoping we could go to town after. I promise you, we will be fine! Look, I even brought you a present." Corjo goes through his bag, which appears new, almost as if he never used it. "I can't find it. I know I brought it, one second." He rips his bag trying to find my gift.

He hands me a thin black book. "Here, it's for you." It was a hard-cover book. The cover is smooth on my fingertips. On the bottom right corner, it had what I imagined was someone's name scratched out.

"You bought a book?"

He nervously laughs. "No, it was my mother's. She found it long ago but never wrote a word; its pages are blank."

"Where is she? I'd like to meet her." The birds fly in a circle as if they are playing tag. Then they glide towards town where the sun shines brighter.

"Not sure. I'd like to meet her as well. When I was around three, she disappeared from my life. To be honest, when I look at your mom, even with her troubles, she's an admirable woman."

My voice rises unexpectedly. "Thank you for the book."

He stares at me. "I want your first story written, and I'll be the first to read it. Corjo sticks his pinky out again I notice his nail chewed low he must have had it for breakfast. "What is it this time Jones?"

"I'm glad I met you, I'll take the risk, and that's a promise." He smiles at me. Our pinkies intertwine with one another and we begin to play chess with. The board is old.

"How many games do you think we played?"

He shrugs. "At least over a hundred, I think." He smirks at me. I know but never state it, however, he was not off by much. More importantly, I think he knew as well.

I begin the game often trying to save my pieces, especially the two powerful rooks. Our strategies always echo each other. "Are you going to push up your knights to free your bishops?" He looks at me with an acute gaze.

"Nope, going with a new approach. You're smarter than you put on." He pushes up his pawns on the corner; two moves up. "Your turn," he says confidently.

The next move I didn't see coming. He snatches a piece. The board shakes and rattles every time a piece lands on a tile. He is focused like an ant trying to avoid getting stomped on. After I swept his queen late in the game, he could make two moves, either sacrifice his rook or his queen. He chooses the rook. "Why didn't you save your queen? She is more useful."

He responds with a question. "Is she though? To me, the rook is an unknown piece. You will never unravel its move until it's too late."

"How's your Pa?" I say. The way he looks at me makes me wish I hadn't.

"He is a man who lost so much and gained nothing. His faith in the Lord rots quickly like a corpse. He became someone who didn't believe in any higher power. I forget what they call those people."

"A lost human is all." I told him, as if I knew. "So what does that make you?" I close my eyes. Tapping on my thigh, he looks up at the clouds wrap his arm around the back of the dark bench. Only a few clouds occupy the sky no wind in sight.

"I can't say for now, but I'll tell you eventually." He shouts, "Check!"

I move a pawn forward. I somehow manage to stall the game.

He looks up at me after his move. "How are you going to start your book? Any ideas on how you might begin?"

"Not sure yet. Margo told me an interesting sentence." I tap on his shoulder to draw his attention from Milo. "Pay attention. She told me, a name without a face is intangible, as a face without a name. I still don't know the exact meaning but have a close idea."

I see Milo in the distance playing in the grass, rolling on his back and scratching. It's funny how fast his little legs were peddling. The sun is shining on his white furry stomach as he licks at the air. He comes over chewing on some twigs and grass. When he barks, the brown grass falls from his mouth. I pet him.

Corjo asks, "What do you think it means?"

I shrug, picking up after my Ma, unintentionally becoming my own personal habit.

Milo starts to bark after the exciting game, even though he did not watch.

"Let's go to town. We have him as our knight, plus he looks bored. Look at him, he's giving you those irresistible eyes."

"It's been a long time, but I suppose nothing will happen if they see me with Corjo. I will keep my eyes sharp and try not to draw unwanted attention." I leave without telling Ma.

The walk to town is no more than a couple minutes. The red fence in the back slowly disappears. Horses wait for their owners, standing in their own filth, their tail shaking off flies. I wonder what they eat.

People hang outside taverns. They wear tan, blue, and green plaid shirts made of cotton. Their sleeves are rolled up. The men are in leather boots and hi-low trekkers. The women wear their hair down. Their breasts are aroused and perked from within black corsets. Brown barrels are on the side of the small building. There are tables outside as men drink and shuffle cards. "No such thing! The wind flipped my card over. I'm not drunk." I overhear a man say. They are sitting on boxes enjoying a card game.

Corjo goes inside and grabs food. It takes him awhile to return. "Have you read her letter yet? It's been awhile since you looked at it," he asks while we are sitting on the ground.

"No, I'm waiting because I'm too scared to discover what she left, her last words. I can't imagine what it could be." I sink my teeth into another bite juice flows out. The hot dog is rich maybe a little chewy like a rubber. He begins to make the loudest and most annoying sound I can think of, his drink finished but he kept trying as if more may come out. "What's your book about? Me right?" The workers circle around Connie's Joint. Picking up plates and glass. Doors swinging open with people leaving and coming to dine.

"It could be, or maybe I already started." I wink at him. He blushes like a cute tomato. The crater on his cheeks burrow.

Corjo bombards me with a series of questions. "Did you pick a title, what's it about, setting. Wait, don't tell me instead surprise me."

Jones bends over and does a whole skit just to surprise his dog with a hotdog. Talking to the furry creature like a baby, I hear him whistle as well. We wait for Milo to finish.

"What you think Ms. Bell's sentence means?" He ask.

"Mhm, maybe something like remembering . . . no more like knowing a loved one face is knowing their physical appearance maybe their flaws and their ability everything you admire about them."

He cuts in, "it's not what they can't do it's the compromise."

"Knowing their name is the history you carry, what does or did that person mean. Why were they your hero."

Milo strangely starts pacing in small circles sniffing the gravel, then he stops looks at us with a satisfactory decision. He hunches his tail erect in the air. One drop of poop hit the ground. "Stop him! He is doing it again!" I panic not trying to get in trouble and not sure what to do so I attempt to stop Milo. I use my bare hands, touching his poop before it falls. The dog's face might well have laughed at me. "It's squsihy." I pout.

"Eww," he screeches, led by a series of sniggers. The smell is worse than horse's waste. "Wow, did you just . . . wow." Consider me and attention friends.

I lift my palm at his face he covers his nose. "Why are you running?" I ask, chasing him. "It's your dog's mess." I want to wipe my hands on his white sleeve.

"I know where you can wash your hands," he says while running.

I follow after him.

"You smell like Milo's butt by the way. Don't think I won't tease you about this." In the far distance, I swear I see him and his pet clap hands.

# Chapter 7

"Does the bottom of your feet hurt from all these pebbles you step on?" He asks as he gazes at my toes.

"No, this is my life and I wouldn't change it. Besides, it feels wonderful. The dirt is warm on my toes. Where are we going?"

"To one of my favorite spots. Most people steer clear because of the beware sign. But it's a safe area." I've never been this far from home or town. It's greener and has a less gravelly path.

We walk pass the first sign stepping over wood chips then over the gates as his dog went underneath his tail straightens out as he rubs against the gate. It shook and made a slight jiggling clank sound.

The path is hidden and the grass shows no trace of people walking over it. Trees are full-grown as we head down a small slope. The creek a long snake wrap around the forest, small rocks float on the bottom. Across is a deer drinking its head jolt when the twig snap between my big toe. It resumed drinking then graze the grass green with flavor.

Corjo jumps in the water with no hesitation. His back shoulder bone like wings on a bird. He has a rash on the valley of his back. "Join me." He splashes around. I don't know who he talking to because Milo spring in. The dogs jump pauses in mid-air just before ripping the water. Tiny rings disperse. "I don't know how to swim!" I yell back while bathing my hands.

I take a seat next to an enormous tree where he left his shirt. Many ropes are attached to the tree as if they were floating balloon strings. The tree is rough when my hand glides across it. I take out my book from his small leather bag with one strap.

We yell back and forth to each other, testing our small knowledge, but it's growing rapidly. Words start to fit like puzzle pieces.

The scenery and smell is mesmerizing. There are lots of trees and birds above my head providing shade but leaving enough light to shine through. I search for a comfortable position. Lying on my stomach hurts; maybe my back will be more soothing.

Clouds slowly approach us, swallowing the sun's light. I read over my notes word by word, only stumbling on a few hard vocabulary words or sentences Bell wrote down. It's like wearing glasses with a broken lens. I only can see certain words; the rest are still blurry.

It gets darker. I look up and see a fleet of ravens glaring at me multiple sounds from their native tongue swimming in the air. Their energy unclear but if anything they brim with bad news. Warning me as if something were to come. To my astonishment, one flew down its cold eyes frighten me a bit. Its narrow wings are flopping. The bird kept hopping around.

Two more join then fly away quickly. It stands out from the others because it has a scar across its beak and below its eyes. We engage in a dual. It opens its beak, looks at Corjo, then flaps away, with enough force to turn my page. I watch as it disappears through the trees.

"Hey, what are you staring at with such passion?" He approaches me with mute footsteps.

"This weird bird flew down. I don't really know what else to say. It was strange."

"The raven? You know they say to stay away from those things. Nothing good comes from them. But my mom used to say ravens serve as a messenger that warns anyone of troubles to come."

"Yeah, that's weird. It's only you and myself here. I guess Milo too." It begins to drizzle. "Maybe this was the warning, the rain. Maybe we should head back," I say, looking at him.

"Yeah we should leave from here, but, first you have to swim with us!" I slap his pinky away not this time Jones but I did not showing any aggression.

"No, I never will. The water is cold. I'm tired of cold." I stomp and kick my feet only to realize he is tugging me towards the water. Milo's sharp bark is in my ear. Without jumping in the water, I feel the coldness waiting lurking for my warm body. "Wait, I cannot swim. Wait I hate water. Corjo stop! Milo help me." I plead.

I jump in. It is not deep until I take more steps, then there is a sudden thud as if someone is jerking me towards the bottom.

"Be careful it's deep over here."

Wish he said that earlier.

He shows me how to float around, then I slowly start to swim in circles looking like Milo. My dress feels like a stuffed pillow, thick with feathers. My mouth accidentally gulps water. The rain hits harder and sounds as if someone is playing a drum using our heads. I shout with glee. Wiping rain from my eyesight, my hair is damp like soggy bread. I don't care that it is pouring; we are having fun.

We decide to leave.

The rain begins to pour harder and faster. My vision becomes weak as we fight our way through the jungle. "My home is a lot closer, did you want to stop there?" he asks.

"I probably shouldn't. My parents are surely worried about me. Tomorrow or another day."

He holds his pinky out and laughs. "Okay. The least I can do is take you home."

We press forward, taking on a new path as we remove a log from our trail into an open road that leads us back into town.

The sky clears and the rain returns to a gentle tap. He mumbles something. I tell him to speak up and repeat his words. "I said my dad won't come home tomorrow so we will be fine. However, he does not hold the kindest of hearts."

"What's that supposed to mean? I'm not sure I understand," I shout.

He kicks his feet. Embarrassment cloaks his visage and says, "he hates people like you. That is why we don't get along."

I don't say much after but I do ask another question I've been holding back since I met him. "Where your shoes?"

"You know where they are—the same place. I haven't worn any since that day." He says with a bold grin.

I know he is hurting because he hops around, relieving the pain from one foot to another. I take action and tie a bundle of thick leaves around his feet using the string I use to put up my hair. Luckily he has a small rope in his bag for his right toes.

"Did that help? Your new footwear. Ma showed me that technique. I call it Abel's special shoes, plus Mama."

"Now that you mention it, yes, thank you."

Halfway through Welton Town, he says, "Sorry, it's getting late so I'll see you soon." He waves goodbye. "Come here Milo, here boy."

If I had to admit it, he did change my views. He is like a lighthouse guiding me through the mist, but the minute I return back home the light is at a distance and is far from my fingertips. I extend myself but unfortunately I'm not blessed; I couldn't reach or climb any higher. One of the reasons why I practice and re-read the same lesson is that sometimes it takes more than prayers.

I run through town, thinking I may get harassed, but luckily no one pays attention. The people hold wet newspapers by their sides or above their heads and some are prepared with dark umbrellas. They are all babies; it's just water.

Home at last. I'm worn out. If I'm this tired, how does Milo feel? His small body always manages to keep up. Like when we take two steps, it's at least five steps for him, poor guy. My stomach pinches with a sharp pain.

Pa and Ma are engaged in what most would think are a foolish act but I understood them, with Ma's weird movements and signs.

"Where have you been?" My humor in all this is, at least only one parent can scold me. I hug Ma and Pa.

"With Corjo."

He interrupts me. "Abel I don't know when but I am positive Margo's husband will make an unexpected visit. I am more than sure Flint told her. I'll continue to pray for us."

The grass and ground dazzle orange, the sun on the horizon.

I open the door to her house. I step in and with a snap of a finger, I feel old memories clashing. The last time I saw her home was the day Flint came. I see the scratch on the floor and the stains I made a long time ago. I begin to open doors, trying to uncover Ms. Bell's secretive home or more like I'm hoping to seek out any clues of her death. The day Flint told us of her demise, it felt like a lie, like he was hiding something. I open the cabinets, drawers, and bedrooms doors. There were enough beds to house all of us including our new addition, who would hopefully join the family soon.

I unlock a black door. It is slightly different from the rest. Ten squeaky steps then a cold blue stone ground. Downstairs, I see what stands as an unfinished area, looking old and sour. The floor is wet and bumpy like small prickly thorns. Water drips from a rusty old pipe in the corner. It smells like my toes, not a good smell either. There are boxes from toe to head filling the room. And there were two doors, one opening into a small bedroom. The other is sealed shut. I don't see any keys lying around. I wonder what's behind it.

I search through the boxes, finding nothing but old photos, mugs, and old empty cartons. I see paper with written words.

I hear a whisper that crawls up my back. "What are you doing here?" Flint is standing in front of me.

I panic. "I . . . I'm looking for something your mother said she left me." I scout the room hunting down my next lie.

"She said to take this box in front of me." I point to it, my hands still shaking. I look away from him, wincing a bit.

Flint steps draw near me. I can hear his boots clicking and sliding across the wet floor. He bends down and mutters, "We raised your father well don't you think? A burly man. He's the perfect stock. Don't you agree? Abel deary." He laughs and grazes past me.

I can breathe again, taking in air as if surfacing from drowning.

He took the oxygen from the room the minute he showed, I'm alone, frightened with a soaking dress and warm thighs. My legs are warm as the yellow liquid drizzle to an open drain.

I start to rummage through the boxes inside. One of them grabs my attention like the words "I love you."

In the shed, I place Bell's letter on top of the safe. On the floor, I lean on a faint gray beam that seems as if it could collapse at any time, thinking about Flint's comment.

# Chapter 8

Have you ever gone without food? Food running low. Mama and Pa sacrifice their food so I can avoid that annoying gnawing your stomach makes. I refuse but they insist.

"Abel eat, stay strong for us," Pa cries. I tell Ma she is carrying our treasure. Her rough bruised hands on my face press hard against my cheeks. Her glow could be related to the small fireplace in Margo's home. She mouths, "Precious Abel."

In our shed, I eat the piece of bread only because I didn't want to see her suffer. A single touch on my face had me succumb to her desires, her only wish. Her belly is plump with my little brother or sister and may need plucking any minute. Ma's personality illuminates my own, often showing me right from wrong in her actions. I have an uneasy feeling about Mama's devotion towards her baby. I believe she would rather let her kid die than have the child breathe in the sins of the world. If life was so unforgiving, my baby sibling could end up in the clutches of someone else and not for the best. Before any of those events can happen, Ma will make the final act—a necessary evil Mamas' are the bringer of life they are not meant as a reaper.

It's odd, I most certainly agree, if I can't live a life without chains or days without fears, what's the point? With questions like that gives rise to another sin, who am I to God—chattel, an item without any say? No! I am more than that. I'm his child, so why? Some answers are best left in the dark as Pa says.

Since Margo passed, life been tougher. There is not enough money for seeds to plant. Ma and Pa still work in the garden in case a miracle should happen, keeping the soil soft for planting. I pull weeds.

I'm waiting patiently for Corjo to escort me to his humble abode. Where is he?

I spot a familiar person in the distance. My stomach gets a funny feeling again and not because I have not eaten a full-size meal. He waves as I do the same.

"Hello," he shouts.

"Hi," I respond. My hands extend, forming into a hug. This boy means a lot to me. I have grown to feel comfortable in his arms. I take off my gloves when he comes closer.

Pa starts talking. "You kids sure are stretching."

Corjo looks at me in question. "He means we are getting taller." I tell my folks goodbye. Ma points to the sky. "Yes I know, back before dark."

When I was younger, I always ran out into the woods and all kinds of places, chasing the animals but I was too slow to keep up. Rabbits are quick. I always came home late. Ma came up with her sign. And I was never late again just so she does not worry. Her face molds into sadness and instantly I know she mad but more worried that I'm out by myself.

We walk past Gazel Road into his home. There is a big tree that shades his house. His house looks like it's been abandoned. The color of the house is a tasteless white, like someone splashed porridge on it. There is broken window glass on the ground but only small pieces. And his front door is brittle with long scratch mark. They look like claws from a beast. In his dusty yard lies small patches of green grass.

"Come in and make yourself a home, also make sure you wipe your feet first."

I laugh. I'm not sure if it was a joke or if he is serious or just being him. "Nice home," I say politely, giving him the same treatment.

"You hungry?"

I told him no. But he had already started cooking.

Corjo has one sofa like Margo. I see one bathroom and two bedrooms. He yells from his kitchen "Sorry about the mess! I'm usually the only one around so I tend to get lazy."

I sit down and eat every bite. His potatoes drench with salt and butter. Small slice of pork green herbs on top drizzle in garlic. I feel guilty eating this much and my Ma and Pa struggling. He made enough for two or maybe three stomachs. "Here try this. It's catchup. Not sure why it spelled differently. People are such idiots."

"I've made some for your parents as well." Blowing on his food. Gold fluid spill when he slice through the meat. Our plate on our laps sitting on his sofa. A piece slips out his mouth. I ripped into the pork. Had no intentions of using a knife. The liquid thick and spicy. Its taste made me want to dance crazy like but I held my urges.

I reply, "I'll take it when I go. I don't plan on staying too long. Thank you for making something for them. The food was delicious." Looking around his living space, his walls are a repulsive yellow color paint with brown stains, almost like how babies smear their hands against the wall. His floorboards have fractures as if a knife was repeatedly dropped on them and they squeak with every other step.

We start talking on his sofa. "For your story you should have a name! Well, you already know that much."

Corjo walks to his kitchen the dish clatter. The draws squeak. He shows me on a paper as he finishes writing it down. "Yeah because you know, you want to write."

I look outside the window, still plenty of daylight left before night eats the sun.

I can see the moon and sun arguing in a kid voice. "It's my turn let me shine, the world needs me." The sun says back "well you slept all night so no!" Says it while he flicks his or her hair, shoulder turn. I think that's why the moon looks so sad.

"Helloooo, Abel. And I'm the clueless one says the girl."

I say the next odd statement. "How come you saved me. You and Milo help me with those vicious kids."

"Not sure. Honestly, can I say I would have done it for anyone? I can't answer that but something took over and led me to you. I saw the huge crowd of kids then your hurt voice overwhelming theirs. I'm glad I stumbled into you. What are you writing now? Can I see?" I've been spotted.

"Oh, my story." I smile cheerfully and close the book he gave me. "So tell me something with wisdom from the brightest youth," he says.

"Shut up." I begin to tap. "Okay. Uhm, hmm, a writer is like a captain. If you believe in a writer, he or she will get you to your destination, as a boat captain does. Authors know how to guide your thoughts through the storm. All I ask is for my crew to stay for the ride. It could get bumpy at first, but, it will smooth out eventually. I need my loyal crewmates as an audience." He starts to clap.

"What?"

He looks at me. "I like it. It should be in a book or something."

"Where's your dad?" I remember what he said about his old man. I should leave soon, as I don't want to get him in trouble. Pa's voice echoes in my ears, don't be a troublesome girl, Abel.

"He left to visit his mom, at least that's what he tells me. He's not coming back till early tomorrow." He stands up and grabs his glass sitting on a small square table in front of us.

He stutters. "I-I-it's okay. We don't talk much. He leaves from time to time, leaving me to raise myself. I know he's going crazy over my mom, wherever she ran off to. My father gave up. He gave up on me and only sought out his desires to drink and to confine himself. Every time I see him with a glass, I have to slap it out of his hands but that doesn't go well." Corjo comes back and hands me my glass. One look inside made me set it down. As he drinks water, it trickles from the side of his face. Standing in front of the window, he shades me from the sun then wipes his mouth with his hand.

He shows me an antique picture of his family. I see a beautiful young woman not much older than my mama maybe younger.

I stare at him. "Tell me more about your Ma. What was she like and what was her name? How did you view her?"

Corjo walks over to a piano in the corner. His beautiful piano appears to be played every day; there is no dust or rust. Jones starts playing the most beautiful sound, notes only angels should hit. There is enough love to remedy a war. My ears draw in, swaying my head with an appealing sound that vibrates the body.

"This is the same song my mother used to play. I don't remember the name of the composer, some old guy from the late 17th century I believe," he continues delving into his past.

"My mom was a woman of many tastes, a rare beauty. Her long brown hair dazzled a crowd. She adored music and shined at the piano, captivating Dad and my heart. We even attended church. Think about it, me strapped in my overalls and Dad sharp as usual in a gray suit and black cap. We walk in as if we own the place, worshipping the good lord. Ever since I lost her, I've played on her instrument. I didn't do it just for me, but, hoping he and I could connect, but I'm afraid."

"What are you afraid of?" I ask.

He starts trembling, inhales steeply with a sigh "Scared that I will soon forget. I remember how her fingertips on the keyboard gave me the illusion that she was moving the stars, giving me access to touch them. Mom, she was so cocky too, smiling at me as if to impress me but she didn't need to. She shone. She was my everything, my queen. Yeah, my undefeated queen. But she's gone, Abel. I never imagined that something so pure could just take off. I often wonder if it was me, but that's a lie because that's how close we were. If she was around, I only wanted to play a song that would never end—to have another chance to stare at her ocean-blue eyes. I might have a picture but that not enough! Without the history, it's meaningless. I was too young. I can't remember the times we had except the music that I once heard that can soothe a beast."

"Tell me her name." I'm still sitting on the couch, the music engulfing my feelings.

"Carla Louise Jones," he forces out of his lips.

"What you just played is very touching," I express to him.

"Thanks. As a kid, she played that all the time. It was our memory, our time. I was her treasure and she kept me safe, held me, and . . . and . . ." He exhales, wanting his mother to ask him what's wrong, wondering if she could hear that sigh. "I miss her." Submerged in an ocean of pain he tries to bottle his tears. His head tilts in a burst of blinking.

I use my sleeves to gently wipe his tears running down his cheeks. He gains his composure as my right arm softly wraps around his shoulders. The music trap me yanking my feelings.

"Some nights I wake up. Most people will get up to use the bathroom or get a glass of water. But me, no, I am up playing. If the tune stops, Mom goes. I kept practicing but at times when her thoughts seep from my grasp I wake up and play. Milo remembers. He curls in a ball with his tiny ears listening, basking in mom's favorite song. I really wish I remember what happened to her." He plays another song, just as beautiful.

"Can you teach me to play?"

He nods.

The first strum sounds like thunder. As I move to the right, the noise goes lighter—from throwing bricks to feathers, like the storm passed.

He points at the keys, "hit here, here, not that one, and here."

I play a brief part of what he just played. He continues to teach me. We slowly lose track of the time. "Wow, you are a quick learner too."

I start to make nonsense noise on the keyboard, but he seems to enjoy it.

We take a seat on his furniture talking. My hands raise as I yawn.

He falls asleep in my lap and I shortly follow. Time fades and so does my caution.

# Chapter 9

"What's that noise?" I ask. "It sounded like keys jingling!"

"No, it's probably just some birds pecking on my broken window or door."

I hear a voice. "Corjo, are you home? I'm back."

I whisper, "What should I do? That's probably your dad."

He swiftly looks around the room then points to a bunch of boxes in the corner. I go over and lie low.

They begin to argue. "Dad, why are you here?" His father speech slurs like Flint. The next thing I know, I hear a thud as if a body sharply fell down.

Exiting the small kitchen, he shouts "You still have that stupid dog around? It reminds me of Carla. I told you to get rid of it, didn't I?"

I hear a drawer open then slam. He stumbles over in Milos direction, just missing me. His eyes are blind with rage and liquor. Mr. Jones opens the door where his pet is lying down in a deep sleep. He grabs the small dog by the neck and lets it hang. Milo is whimpering, his pain surrounds the house. " I don't like it. I never did."

"Milo did nothing to you. Let him go!" A gun fires and Milo is on the ground. They continue to fight. Mr. Jones and his son. Corjo lands a good punch but his father retaliates and hits him twice on his head with the pistol.

The back of my throat itches. My hands are damp even though I wipe them on my dress. I don't know why but I race to the back door. I grab the knob but its locked. I start to intensely shake, trying to pry the door. The twitching of the knob screeches in my ear.

"Who's over there?" I hear his father shout.

I get up not thinking. I charge towards him. I bump into his round belly. I inhale the smell of alcohol and sweets.

"Hello, I'm Abel," I say nervously, my left hand rubbing against my right as if I were cold. I can tell he is not happy to see me, gripping his gun even harder. His face is turning like a rotten tomato. The thickness of his nostrils flares revealing his accumulated nose hairs.

"Dad, dad, stop. What are you doing? She is my friend!" I slowly back towards his kitchen, hoping to run for the door. His set of keys clangs together with each step he takes toward me.

"First, you disgrace me and now this. Look at this . . . this thing is disgusting! They should all just die! I'll be doing the world a favor." His bushy hands grab me by the hair then quickly by my throat. The air in the room vanishes. Corjo knocks him off as he topples gaining his balance before kissing the floor.

"Leave her alone. Why can't you ever be like mom? How did I shame you? Talk to me! You never do."

The air came rushing back. I run for the door then jerk it. The door collapses, pinning me. He points the gun at my head, the metallic click springing then he hesitates. Corjo jumps at his father, climbing on his back so his weapon fumbles. Mr. Jones shoves his son, knocking him into a countertop. I struggle to get the door off me.

He snatches me by the foot. His hands are all over me, places that were unforgivable. "Where do you think you're going?" I start to scream and scream. His aggressive body dominates my own. His hands cover my mouth, muffling my voice. I bite with force to cut a raw meat but he punches me for my defiance. I cry, not being able to get him off. The strap of my dress pulls near my chest. His moan creeps up my leg. I thrash around like a dying fish. He has long forgotten where his gun was and proceeds towards me with a new intent. I lie down helplessly.

I spot a knife on the ground and stretched for it. I take a lethal plunge and stab him in three different spots. The last stab is below his shoulder. I fly out the house, screaming in alarm even though no one is in sight. Not looking back, I head home.

When I open the shed doors, I see Pa hovering over Ma. Her back is on the mattress with a wet towel on her head.

I pause on my life and what happened. "Mama what's wrong?"I ask after her aggressive cough. Her stomach rumbles and ripples. She seems ill from the lack of food.

"Your ma is doing well," Pa says. "Time for your sister or brother." His hand firmly holds Mama's. A sense of relief surfaces, especially feeling guilty after eating. A quick thought arrives. I spring into action.

Inside Margo's home, I decide to search. Maybe I can find some food or anything to help. I destroy her house. I look in her cabinets, top and lower shelves but nothing. Open some tin cans still no luck.

I did find towels for Mama. Just when I was about to give up, I decide to look into the door behind Margo's sewn stand. It's small. "God bless you." A shipment of food. Canned goods, rice, beans, corn, and more.

"What are you waiting for? Eat," I say, handing them food. Mama is still sweating on the bed. Pa walks to her, squeezing water out of a cloth.

"We will eat when the baby eats," he says. I insist we go inside.

The door slams closed. A heavy wind presses against it. "Pa, please let's go inside. I know you rather stay out here." They stare at each other, then Mama nods. Pa gently wraps his hands under her legs and upper back. Her blanket is still on her. Pa and Ma wait on me.

"Abel," he grunts. Mama shrieks in pain. The door became heavy to open.

We lay Mama on Margo's soft mattress. Her room is just like her. Her blanket is folded with two dark pillows.

Tears escape their eyes. "What's her name, Abel?" Pa asks.

I take my younger sister in my arms. I use a white cloth to wrap around her tiny body. "Ina."

# Chapter 10

Ina is a gift from above. Every time I hold her, I instantly fill with blissful emotions. Yet I feel scared that I may drop her.

Ma and Pa are asleep. Ina and I are talking, well, I'm doing most of the talking. She just sits, looking around the room aimlessly.

I start thinking about Margo. "Now, I know Ina dear, you would have been fond of her. She had a kind heart I was stupid to think otherwise. I remember how we sat at her table and spent times spelling her name. I never could get it right but finally did. She owned this black quill pen that she always used." Ina starts what might be a giggle. Her cheeks are soft and warm. I feel a bit chilly sitting on the couch so I start a fire.

"When Margo finished, I started to write, mocking every stroke she made. When you start writing, watch out for w's; they are not at all like the letter u. They are more like double v's. I remember every time I wanted to sneak past the table she stopped me. Especially when I reach for the basement door. She'd say, Sit down Abel. She told me to stay focused and stop fussing around—a tough old woman that's for sure. Her voice never did fit her appearance." My face twists to make her laugh. It doesn't work.

"Bell told me stories about New York. New York sounds just like the papers I find fluttering through town, hoping to latch onto a host to glance at its pages. She promised me one day she would be my escort. Margo never did talk about her husband or her family. However, she did say she loved that man. She looked worried when I mentioned him; she never did give me a name, except she called him a donkey, shh you did not hear me cuss. Margo was so funny that way."

My lap tingled from her sitting too long. I toss her on my arm. Her body squirms. "All right, stay on the couch. Didn't want to hold you anyways." Ina gazes at the fire, her brown eyes sparkling. Her hands reach towards it with such mystery. The wood cracks and spits.

"One of my favorite memories with her is one special night she read to me. Flint was gone and Margo welcomed us in. I think I was seven at the time. I remember crawling underneath the covers next to her and she read. We read all night, whether fiction or historical, she had a fascinating way to narrate a story. I could tell each emotion a character is or was feeling. I loved that about her. How could I have been so . . . so unwilling to forgive? She was nothing but honest. You know what else, she had a wisdom of ten men put together." I flex a muscle. "Since I didn't learn how to read until a later age, I always paid attention to how she acted. The way she moved, the way she carried herself, and most importantly the way she spoke. Bell was always so art . . . excuse me, I cannot remember the word she uses. Articulate, that's it. I remember how she always wielded her word like a weapon."

"We took a carriage into town. There is this great place for pastries and other goods. Also, she had this one friend she introduced to me. I received the usual looks at first, but I think she came around unless she was excellent at faking her kindness. What was her name again? I want to say, Betty, she looked like one anyway. Betty owned a very small flower shop. They talked up a storm when they crossed eyes. I didn't say much around other people, maybe fear or something simpler. I did not like them. She never did attempt to get to know me but I was always on my best behavior never gave anyone a reason to act bitter. Honestly, though, I think bell smacked anyone if they ever frowned at me. She always helped us support the garden, teaching us how to keep the crop alive and fresh."

"It bothers me that we never stayed in the house. Flint denied us access and Pa didn't want to disturb. He said it will be easier for everyone, of course, Margo had a say but couldn't change Pa's mind."

I can tell Ina is listening to every word. "Finally, I have your attention I see." Her face is droopy.

There is a weird knock from the door. Not the usual pounding. I carefully throw myself towards the door, thinking the worst. I stumble on my words, "W-who . . . there?" Silence. Another knock. I crack the decorative door, my heart racing faster than a horse in the wild. "Hello? Anyone there?" I say, searching.

An envelope? I flip it over and I realize it's Bell's last words to me. Who left it here? I turn my head left then right. If a soul is around, I would have seen them.

Kraa, kraa, caw. The moment I look up, I'm acquainted with a scarred raven—one across the beak and below its tiny eyes flying away like before. I remember the envelope in the shed.

I stand there staring at the letter halfway in and out the house, confused on what should be done. Should I open it? I know I'm ready. I think. I begin to tear off the corner. I notice my hand is shaking with moist. I pull the letter out and begin to read. "Dear Abel." Ina begins to cry so I set the letter down.

I hold my baby sister. Her eyes resemble Ma's, big and brown. Ina's nose is definitely Pa's. She smiles and giggles. I poke her belly for amusement; it's softer than warm bread. I kiss her on the forehead multiple times and whisper, "I will never let anything happen to you." I continue telling her stories, this time about Corjo. My whole body stretches on the floor and she is on my stomach.

Ma comes out the bedroom. I see her glow has returned. She looks at me, then the wall where the entrance is. "No one Ma." Momma walks over, bends down and kisses the two of us. She gives me a look that seems like she heard me talking earlier and wants me to resume. I swear I saw her ears rise up like a Milo's waiting for their meal.

"Okay." I start telling a Corjo tale. Not knowing if he is safe is troubling me. I calm myself trying to remember something. Ma is feeding her baby on the sofa. Her hair is wild from sleep. Mama taps on her head. "Yes Ma, I'll go get your cloth."

Ina is buried in Ma's lap sleeping. She pats the sofa, noting a hiss out like at Corjo. The fire and wood become more lively, making more noise than before. I see black ash in the air.

I tell Ma who destroyed the church. "It was a group of clan members that came by. I'm not sure on the details but sheriff's discovered their whereabouts. "They are locked up Ma!" They are elsewhere because the nearest jail cell in another town. I see her leaning in for a hug. It tough, the two people she ever talked to . . . well communicated with besides Pa and I we don't see much of. They were two women that were basically Mama's sister the way they acted. African sisters thickest of accent and filled with pride. It's hard finding someone who doesn't think she is a burden and can take the time to learn or cope with her.

I used to love running around the church with the other kids. We would run and push each other However, nobody is near as close a friend as Corjo.

"Momma you're hurting my hair!" She picks at it as if she's creating a masterpiece. Honestly, I like how my natural hair is. The kinks come and go. She has never had the right touch to make it less painful. It's like she is pulling weeds or something tougher.

I bring back a past memory of Ma and myself. I always hated washing clothes and she knew it too. Ma exerts a little chuckle. "Softer Ma!" She hits me below the chin, with four fingers—her signature, meaning stop fussing. But Pa gets it when he asks a silly question.

It was always my job to get the small wooden bucket with two handles on each side. We grab some water from the creek. I hold the bucket on my head, trying to do as she does. We hum her favorite song. By the time we get back, I look like I took a dip in the water head first.

We finally scrub our clothes on a washboard that grinds at my fingers. There is nothing fun about washing clothes. I scrub and scrub but nothing seems to work then she comes and shows me up. By the time we finish, I have lines on the tip of my fingers like wrinkles and I'm not even that old. Momma dries and I wash; it's the cycle we have. I love how she hums this song that always makes me feel like I'm vanishing elsewhere. When she starts, my mind draws a blank. I don't remember washing clothes! It feels as if I am lying down in a field of flowers, letting the day escape. I can almost hear her voice through her song; it's clear like the sky. We hang the clothes on a string that is tied from Bell's home to the big tree.

I feel Ma's warm palm on my face. "I love you, Mama."

The baby wakes. Ma thrusts her arms in a back and forward motion, rocking her child, my sister. "Hi, Ina. Can I try Ma?"

I figure I should go see if Corjo is all right tomorrow. For the time being, I wish to absorb my family's company.

# Chapter 11

Where does he live? I take a deep relieved breath when I finally see Gazel Road. I arrive at his home, picking unwanted rocks and dirt from my feet. Every step feels like climbing a mountain. It has suddenly become cold, so cold.

I hesitate, drawing my hands back before knocking. His dad could...No! I have to stay strong. I walk away, hoping something will turn me around. Nothing does, but the urge to see him overshadows my weakness.

I quietly knock on his door—three quick bursts and nothing more. In the back of my mind, I am really hoping nobody is home. There is a long pause after my knock. Just when I decide to take my leave, the door slowly opens; the creak rings in my ear.

"Hi. How are you?" I ask cheerfully but with strong concern. I stare at him as if sculpting an ice sculpture and admiring my work. I do not want to do or say anything wrong. The atmosphere feels delicate but tense.

Corjo walks away, not making a splash of eye contact.

"What's wrong?"

"It took you twenty-one days to check on me?"

"Sorry, I couldn't . . . I . . . I was scared. Your dad."

He walks past his room into the living area.

"You know, I worried about you," he says.

Corjo continues to his old-looking couch with puncture holes and taps on the cushion next to him, but on the opposite end.

When the light shines through his window, I see a bandage wrapped around his head.

"I'm glad you're okay," I say gently.

"I'm well." His smile is as fake as it gets. "Abel can I ask you something before I forget?"

"What?"

"How are you doing?"

I sigh in relief, seeing I still have my friend. "I'm fine. Ma gave birth to a girl! She is so beautiful. I want you to meet my sister, your new friend. I know you always wanted a sister. Think of her as one."

"What's her name?"

"Ina. She giggles almost as much as us." I smile. Then I feel my lips moving again. "What did you mean when you said before I forget?"

He gives off a concerned grin. "Doctors say I will have memory loss. They say it's fine for now but eventually, it will get worse or fade. Not sure."

"I don't understand."

"My father . . ." He exhales. "I wish that were the first time he struck me."

I place my palm slowly around his head then down his arm. "I'm sorry, Corjo. I should never have come in the first place." Why won't he look at me?

"Abel D. Bloom, do you remember when you asked me if I took after my father's beliefs?"

"Yeah, why? You said you couldn't tell me until I heard your story about your mother or dad right? Whatever it is, I will not change my mind about you."

"I know."

A noticeable weight flees from my chest after his words.

"My answer to your question is, the apple doesn't fall far from the tree. At least, that's what I believe."

"What does that mean?"

"Oh, nothing. It's just, he didn't use to be like that. At supper, Dad would always say, 'God almighty, please watch over the Jones, especially my boy.' My dad would look at me, then we would all say amen. Would you believe my dad, mom and me held hands together while we prayed like a normal family? It's funny, Dad was the cook."

"Where are your father and Milo?"

"Not around."Corjo looks at me. "Hey, Abel."

"Why are you tearing up?"

"My dad, did...did...he hurt you?" His voice is softer.

"No...well...maybe...I mean, yes."

His face looks as if it is about to burst, his emotions overflowing in a tight balloon that's at its bursting point. One more huff of air, then pop!

"Why are you lying to me? I want to know why."

I clear my dry throat. It almost hurts to swallow. "Corjo, I'm not lying."

"I don't believe you. Then why?" Corjo is breathing hard I can see his nostril flaring.

"Why? Talk to me, . Say something!" The sadness continues."Is it Milo?"

"Milo," he repeats.

I stare at him, and for a minute, not one word escapes our lips.

"Remember what I said about a writer and a captain?" There was no answer in return. The room is in a stalemate. "I said you have to trust and believe in them, now I need you to do the same, Corjo."

"I want to believe you. I do. But remember, I know you so well, we've been through a lot, so—"

I rudely interrupt. "Then why won't you believe me?"

He continues to gaze at the wall and sob.

"Okay, I'll ask once more." He makes a grunting sigh. "Did my father rape you?"

I don't know what to do or say.

"What are you doing?" he asks.

For the first time ever, I put my pinky out first. "The absolute truth, right? That's what you taught me to remember." My voice cracks with violent pain. "Remember, Jones? Absolute truth."

There is a sudden twitch from his arm, but something keeps him from reaching further. He stops from connecting with me, but I keep my left hand hanging in the air for a sliver of hope.

" You believe me, don't you, Corjo?" I ask softly.

His contest with the wall ceases, but his sorrow runs like a stream.

"I know you well, too. Right! Right? Corjo!" I roar, making sure he hears me.

"Where did you get those bruises?" He scans my body.

"I wouldn't lie to you, you have to know that."

He looks up at me with a frozen glare, enough to stall time itself. "Then why was my father lying on the ground with a knife through his arm?"

"I don't know, he scared me. I do remember stabbing him, but it was below the shoulder." I grab Jones by the face bumping forehead and I drift in his brown, glassy eyes.

"So, you did lie?" Those words pull me away from him.

I don't say anything. At last, I say, "Some secrets are best left in the dark."

His expression is one of confusion, but it did not give him ease. He gets to his feet. "Look, my uncle will return shortly. He has Milo. I think you should go."

I do as he instructs. "If you don't want to see me, I completely understand. But, if not for me, maybe my sister, please."

I take my leave and walk back home. The sunny weather mocks me; it does not feel the way I do.

Pa and Ma are up searching the home for cooking materials when I get home. There are loud noises from pots being hurled around.

I walk to my sister. Her eyes are wide open. She is wearing some oversized shirt and smells like Papa. "Hi!" I say to Ina. Mama just stares at me. I wish I could talk to Mama. I lie down next to my sister and before I know it I fall asleep.

When I wake up, I take Ina outside and place her next to me on the bench. I start moving the chess board, showing her pieces of the game. I hear footsteps in the wind like someone is slowly approaching.

"Corjo!" I turn around but there's only empty silence. The next day, I grab my sister and carry her to the same spot. Each day seems like the previous. Every time I hear the sound of footsteps, I look back, but it is pointless. My heart begins to ache at my mind playing tricks on me.

The following day, the sun is going down and Ina is asleep within my arms after I talked her ears off about my problems.

The wind lets out a soft whisper, "Is that her?"

I do not turn around because I don't want it to hurt anymore from the constant rejections, but a shadow stands tall and odorless.

"I wanted to say hi to her."

Ina starts to make noises, letting us know she is waking up.

"Hi. Hi, Ina. I'm Corjo!" They both stare at one another, pleased.

He looks at me and says, "She's so adorable. How could I not come? Allow me to apologize for taking so long." Corjo stares at her with transparent eyes.

"However, I came here to tell you goodbye. He strangely starts setting up the chess board. "Lets play one last game Abel."

Ina sits up on his lap, she is annoyingly touching our pieces. "My dad is recovering, doing better. I wanted to let you know. When I get a bit older, I will move back at the snap of my finger. Let's meet up in, I don't know, four or five years. Less, if possible." At first I find myself speechless. He serious. I was waiting for a joke but Corjo leaving?

I look at him like he is speaking a new language. "How do you know that nothing will happen? How will we meet again? What if I move and can't come back?"

He looks at the sky. It's lonely, with no clouds or birds. "You know our stars align. Your name says it all."

"Okay, okay, you don't have to say any more. Besides, my middle name never felt like it was believing in faith or what-not."

The chess game is intense, and I continue to absorb the rightly placed illusion. "Can I ask you something, Jones?" His chin perks up giving me his full attention. "Anything."

I wait until he finishes making his move.

He yells, "Wait, I didn't want my bishop to move there. Can I take it back?"

"Why?"

He looks at me and whispers, "Because your sister distract-ed me. Just look at her, so cute."

I let him take his move back, only to realize his strategy is better than  my own.

We continue playing; it's drawing to a bitter end. The board draws on no more strength.

"I want to come to New York with you one day. I will con-tinue studying, maybe playing the piano. We could . . . I don't know, be together."

"Looks like you win! Wow, someone actually won instead of a stalemate." We look up.

He places his hands on my face only to slip past me. "One last question, Abel. If my memory is so fragile that you slip beyond my grasp, would you...would I..."

Ina's head rocks back and forth, staring at us both. Her fin-ger clutches her mouth. "Yes, we will always be...real Righters?"

He says, "No, you idiot." He laughs enough to swallow my sorrow.

We head to the house. I wave, and he roams away. Ina is on my hip. Sure, he cried. He couldn't hide it. Did I? No, I didn't. The wind picks up and he is gone, leaving no trace.

I wake up, realizing I have dozed off. I only wish to see him again. I can't shed another tear. The whisper disappears, the wind stops, and the grass is still. When I stand up, the bench shakes and pieces fall off the board of life. Only two rooks were left. The others had perished to the ground.

# Chapter 12

My story continues.

Braxton takes Ina and me to an auction in Savannah, Georgia, leaving Ma and Pa watching us from behind Margo's door.

I pray that what Braxton's friend said was a lie. I don't scream. How can I? The words he said run loosely in my head. My mouth tastes of vomit.

I fade in and out. Ina is in my lap, her eyes shut. Braxton is riding next to our captor being pulled by two brown spotted horses.

He is right about one thing, I don't speak a word. My mind is a blank board, only drawn back when Ina makes a sound. I silently cry in their stagecoach. Passing through the town, it's full of people. I could scream but fear freezes me. My voice has long since disappeared. The stagecoach is rocking back and forth. Both men are loud with laughter and conversation.

They stop at another house. The house is a wooden structure with an unpolished stone chimney. Braxton stays behind and watches my every move. His friend walks over dead grass.

"Abel, don't look so scared. I won't harm you." His match sparks a cigar. Cigar smoke clouds the stagecoach. I face Ina nose toward my chest.

It takes the slave handler but a moment to come out with three other negroes in front of him. He yells at a white family then pushes the youngest boy. Their Ma or older sister has her hair wrapped like Mama's. She is a darker shade with a slim body. Her hips are wide. Both boys have crusty noses. They are young. They haven't even lived yet. Now they are being dragged from their home and will soon be torn apart. It's a sad tale.

"All right. That's the last of em," says the handler. He shoves them on the other side, then climbs up to the reins. "Don't make any fuss! We are full and don't need no problems with the wheels. Hyahh!" He whips the horses and we move, sending Ma and Pa even farther away.

Of course, the kids are scared but I can see they still have hope. But eventually, I have a feeling it will get snuffed out.

I'm thinking about Ma and Pa. I know they won't do anything to harm themselves.

Ina cries for a couple hours of our nightmare journey. I notice she is looking at me for comfort.

"Shut her up now All that unnecessary noise." They both shout. The rope slaps, making the stagecoach go faster. Both horses neigh. Ina doesn't quit with her baby noises. "Here, child. Gimme that baby," says the oldest woman.

I hesitate.

"It be a'right. Now, here."

I hand Ina over and she rocks Ina back and forth while do-ing god knows what else, but it works.

The woman whispers, "Who child this be?"

I don't say anything.

 "How old are you, girl?"

"Fourteen."

After exhausting hours of traveling, we arrive. They toss us, collect their money, and go their own way.

"Take care of yourself." That's the last time I hear his foul voice. How can he do this to us?

The whites house us in sheds, packing us all together. Every day, people come through to look at us, choosing which of us are ripe to pluck. As the whites come, they always examine us or ask questions about our health.

"He looks sick, honey. Maybe him over there."

Two white families are in my cell. Unlike us, they are splen-didly dressed. The woman fans herself as her husband inspects us.

They tell me to open my mouth and check my teeth. The whites are brutal when examining the black males, making sure they are in good shape. I don't feel like a human. We are merely tools.

The shed is small, musty, and disgusting. The air is unbearable. The ground is damp with golden straw. We use the large
haystack in the corner to sleep on. It's cold. I try my best to
keep my sister warm.

"Eat." Men in bright red vests are going around with bowls.

I run to the food, reaching for a bowl. Ina is crying in my
arms and I'm desperately fighting a hopeless battle against the
crowd of adults for food. I find myself shoved in the back. I
sit down, waiting.

There is barely any porridge left when I finally make it to
the front of the line. I break off the stale bread and feed it to
Ina. I take a small nibble, only enough to keep my stomach
from arguing with me all night.

Like Mama, I rock Ina. Across from me, I see the two crusty
boys. They huddle like us.

The next day there is poop and pee on the floor as nobody
cleaned up after the sick. It is loud as a parade as the buyers
watch our every mood.

"Flex your muscles for me, boy." That is all they say—never
asking, always commanding. They ask the women how many
children they have born and if they are currently with child.
Ina is like me—quiet, scared, wanting to be home, and held by
Ma and Pa one more time.

I overhear some people stating their strong points. "Massa,
I'd be a good pick for you, help you bring in much money,
much. Great rice planter! Cotton picker faster you laid eyes
on!" They tell them all kinds of things, just to keep their family
together.

"I real good with a hammer, build you nice hut if yous like. Buy my whole family. My wife and chillen, we together. Please sir, ma'am?"

The woman says, "I cooks all kinds of meal, just name it. But my babies, please don't take 'em away."

Only a few whites come in the cell with us. Others observe from the outside.

Every day, they hose the flock of us. My stomach is hurting from lack of food and sleep. The babies and children are crying. I cry with them but in silence. Everyone is frantic, scared, alone, or worried.

"Don't worry, Ina. I'm still here."

She smiles. I forgot how a smile looks or even makes someone feel.

"Food. Food." This time, a woman's voice. Around her hip is a long leather whip.

A few people come my way, demanding that I bend over, to check for any bruises or anything that may slow my work. They ask if I'm any good at cleaning or looking after children. Can I cook? It is like this for at least four nights and days of torment.

On day three, a clumsy white man wearing glasses comes to ask me questions. "What's your name? It's okay. I'm a friendly face."

He looks exactly like the rest.

"What's your name?" he asks, slightly kinder.

I respond with my sister clutched to my side, "Abel Bloom, sir."

He goes on. "I'm an editor of the New York Daily Tribune and I am here to write about this atrocity that been going on for far too long. I'm going to expose the cruelty that we Americans have had your people endure. My boss, Horace Greeley, sent me to get a few words in."

I nod in agreement.

"Where are you from?" His voice is small, like a woman's.

"Missouri. A small town called Welton, not too far from Jefferson City, sir."

He writes some stuff down and continues. "Is this your child?"

I look behind him, where the whites are aggressively shoving a small boy around.

"My sister, sir. We're separated from my parents. I'm . . . no, we are both free!"

His eyes flicker as his bushy brows raise. He pushes his glasses back. "You seem educated,

I try to reason with him to show he is not mistaken. He is my only chance to get out. I give him what he wants to hear to prove that I'm somewhat educated. "I may not be as strong an intellect as yourself, but I was taught how to read and write and I hone my skills."

Henry is amused that I understood almost every word he said. "My, you're a breath of fresh air, Abel, and you're articulate too. Thank you. I have to go now." His hat falls.

I take it. "Wait, w-wh-what about us? Ma and Pa are worried sick. We have to get back home. Can you take us back?"

"Abel, my hat." His soft hand is stuck out. "I cannot do much now. Give us some time."

He acts as if he did me a favor. As if I was in the wrong!

More people come in, with eyes that suggest they have no interest in our wellbeing but instead, what can we do for them.

"You're heating up." I spare my share to Ina. The poor child will only take a few fingers full.

"My baby, my baby. Someone help him!" The child appears ill and might not survive. His ribcage protrudes through his body.

The whites come in with masks around their noses. We are sprayed with more cold water without warning.

At night I hear singing in different native tongue. I'm not sure what they are saying, but I have my own music and hum it to Ina.

A father and daughter sit next to me. I overhear him talking. "We will meet Mama soon. Okay, Penny? She is in the other cage. When we all together—" He stops, a trickle of tears falling down his face.

My heart aches. He doesn't believe his own words.

"Papa, what's wrong?" she asks. The little girl is maybe nine, clenching her Pa as if he were dying. She swells with sobs. "We are going to get through this," she whispers.

Her words hit me harder because she does believe. Her words hurt even more, even I know. Is it wrong to have no faith?

*March of 1859*

It is day one of the auction and the whites line us up, but only the healthiest of slaves are taken to the platform, led by one of our own. They dress him like a white man—a blue vest with a dark coat. His black shoes match the feather on his hat.

The announcer states, "Ladies and gentlemen of the privilege, good afternoon. I am delighted to see we have people from Georgia, Virginia, the Carolinas, Alabama, and Louisiana. This is one of the biggest sales consisting of four hundred thirty-six slaves. Bid wisely, now. Pick the one most suited to your tastes. The men are sturdy for a day's work. Their arms are big for carrying logs. You name it. The women are passionate for house duties, raising children. The young ones' minds are not yet molded. In other words, they are not as stubborn."

There is a roar of laughter.

I see the woman from the stagecoach and think of the suffering she must be going through. My heart aches for them, for her kin.

"Go girl, you up. Take the baby with you."

My turn. I hold Ina on the platform.

"Last call. Four hundred. Lady in the pink, keep that paddle up. Gentleman in the blue. I see your hand."

"I want her, but only the young lady. The baby can go elsewhere, for all I please! Five hundred eighteen!"

My worth as a human.

# Chapter 13

Corjo

"I think you should go."

The door slowly closes behind her, taking the scent of summer.

"Wait! Abel, come back!" Why did I say those words? The taste in my mouth is awful. Why did I tell her to go?

The last thing I see is the back of her tan blouse and blue skirt, the one that has a small rip at her knee. Her eyes never did stop piercing through my soul, and that is why I couldn't bear to look at her. My own selfish ways. If I want her to return, then why are my legs still attached to the sofa? I place my hand over my head, angry at my ignorance.

This house is more of a mess. I lose it.

"Mother?"

I walk to my room. It feels revoltingly empty. Usually, I see Milo on the floor lying down on the newspaper I lay down after reading. Outside, the grass is still. It's funny, I still hear his bark. He is soft like a stuffed animal but aggressive when he's in his protective mode. I marked his grave with wood from the piano. Maybe he is still listening. My pet since I was a baby, torn from me like my mother was. The more I force myself to remember, the harder it becomes, unbearable. I take the only logical step that can help.

The next day, I hear a knock on my door. Please be Abel, please be her. I hope she doesn't think poorly of me. I hate how we fought and I told her to leave. Why did I say that? I didn't want to tell her to leave, but the words escaped my lips before I could drag them back.

"Corjo! Are you ready?"

It's my uncle. He reminds me of my father—a questionable figure that dominates my actions. He has short, stubby arms with the smallest amount of brown hair to show. He is missing his bottom tooth too, but unlike my father, he is a gentleman.

"Are you packed? Corjo, open the door."

I slug my body towards my bags. My arms lean to the right as I carry both bag. "That looks heavy. Here, allow me."

Uncle smells nice after he hugs me, the smell of honey. "Don't worry. You will be back within a month or so. How are you feeling, pal? I know how much you loved Milo—that's the only reason I let you stay here by yourself. Your father hasn't been the same. Also, did you talk to that friend you so desperately begged to stay for?"

His attention is focused on the road. He stops for a family crossing the street, heading toward Buns and Laugh, a local toy shop. Two blocks over is one of my finest memories of Abel and Milo. I can't believe she touched his poop. I try to smile but can't quite manage it.

"Hey, Corjo? Did you?" Uncle nudges me.

"You should ask your brother, Uncle Sam. He's the one who hurt the dog in the first place."

His thin brow raises with a concerned look but he faces forward shortly after. I hear heavy breathing from him. Almost like he is out of breath.

Uncle's home is several miles away from Welton Town in Cunan City. He is a wealthy man, not insanely rich, but he does well. He is a carpenter. I believe he built his own house. I suppose that's another reason Father is a sour man. I step out of the coach.

"Good morning, Corjo." My cousin Sadie comes outside, trying to help with my bag. She grabs the lightest one, as she already grunted attempting the other.

"Your room is already set up. Your aunt and younger cousin have prepared it for you," Sam says, adding, "Wipe your feet."

My mind is still cloudy and confused. Why do I feel this way? My emotions are gurgling from the bottom of my stomach, ready to explode.

"Corjo, what's wrong?" Sadie asks.

I do not realize how I look. My head is usually held up but it feels heavy.

"I'm fine. Sorry, thinking about my dad," I lie.

When I open the door, their sofa encircles a small square table with a red flower vase on top. I do not notice where their kitchen and living space cut off at. It's one big room. They have a table for eating in their kitchen, like Abel does. On the left wall, there are two shelves. Aunt knits, so she has her equipment on the other side. Heading up the stairs, I make sure I don't trip on toys.

I yell back down. "I'm going to unpack, Uncle."

"Corjo, do you need anything?" Sadie asks.

"Leave me alone. Can't you see I'm studying?"

She flinches.

I stare at the window and see her small reflection. Is she shaking because of me?"

"Sorry, Jones. I did not mean to yell. My mind is cluttered at the moment."

"It's okay, and it's Sadie Walsh. Well, anyways, Mommy says Walsh up for supper. Get it!" She laughs at her joke. The door closes behind her. She can barely reach the knob. She has short blonde hair like boys her age.

I rub my eyes and sit down for a minute. The room smells stale. There is no indication that someone lives in it. My butt hurts from sitting on this wooden chair. There is a desk in front of me. Behind me is my mattress and a bookshelf.

Uncle Sam has plenty of books to read, so those will occupy my thoughts. I rummage through the desk. I have found something to write with. As I read, I write, waiting for the final supper warning. I can only push my luck so far before they get upset.

"Corjo Denzel Jones!" Aunt Lydia calls. That will do it.

"Here I come!" I hurry down the steps. I shake the whole house with my loud footsteps.

"Be careful, Corjo." Aunty sprints and helps me up.

"Thank you."

"Sadie, pick up your mess."

Sadie apologizes.

"Ah" Uncle smacks my hand from the food. "Go wash your hands. Uncle says sternly. They point me toward the bathroom under the steps in a narrow hall.

I douse my whole head in the basin. The coolness feels great on my hair. Glaring at the mirror, a glimpse of my face reveals what Abel calls a "lost human."

Sadie is playing with her food. She hates eating healthy. I'm surprised because she is bone thin. We have a bowl of salad in the center of the table with half cut tomatoes and onion. There is a platter of ribs roasted in honey, peppers, and herbs, one of my favorites. The brown gravy is next to Sadie and I. Across from us are the mashed potatoes, near where Aunty is. Butter is at the head of the table as Uncle slathers butter on the side of his plate.

Silverware and glasses clink and scrape. "Pass the gravy. Also, that jar of salt." Uncle says. "Not too bad honey."

To my surprise, the ribs are delicious. Aunty is not the best at cooking.

"Stop eating. We have to say grace." Sadie says. A piece of meat is hanging from my mouth, the sweet taste of honey dangling on my lips. I contemplate whether I should eat it or not. I give her an annoyed glance.

"Corjo, hold my hands." Sadie says.

"Amen."

Something that stands out is their table, big enough to fit a family. Now this feels like a home—a mother, dad, and their child. I long for those days. Father stopped cooking and expected me to take care of him and myself.

The Walsh's have paintings in each corner. Below our feet is a rug but other than that, it's wood. The house is clean from floor to ceiling.

Even though we have plenty to eat, it does not measure up to the mealtime I had with the Blooms. I understand why I couldn't talk to Abel's mother, but I still want to know her name. She was sweet and caring. I can tell how much she loves her daughter.

"Tomorrow, Uncle Connor comes here. Right, Mommy?"

It feels like someone splashed piping hot water on me.

"Yes, Sadie" She looks at Uncle "my brother is coming. Hey Corjo, after supper I'd like to show you something." Uncle sucks  juice off his fingers.

His ribs are drenched in gravy. I hear hungry mouths devouring a well-presented meal.

In his study, he pulls out a small black box and hands it to me. "Yes, it's your mother's. The same necklace she wore when she drowned. Your father told me to hold onto it till you needed it and I think that time is now."

I hastily take it out. That's right, she did drown. How did I not know? I'm the reason, no wonder he hates me, but why didn't he tell me?

"Careful," he says.

I crouch down, hovering my finger over the necklace. For a moment, I stand there with Mom. "Thank you, Uncle."

He returns to some important looking papers. I forgot what else he does besides his carpentry job.

Aunt Lydia is knitting on her brown sofa. Their home shines with candles that look like healthy carrots set in every room.

"That looks nice on you, dear. That silver shines when it's on you."

"Thank you."

Aunt Lydia is beautiful. She reminds me of Mom. She is wearing white socks, looking cozy. Aunt's wedding band is gold, like her and Sadie's hair.

Her gaze is focused on her wool and thread. I sit by her, trying to keep up with her movements, my eyes swimming. She is quick with her knitting, like a fox sprinting through its natural habitat.

Aunty has dimples like me. I think Abel calls them small craters.

"Want to try?" she asks. Surprisingly, I do. I pick up her basket and set it on the sofa between us.

Step by step, she shows me. "Quick learner," she says. Lydia is being nice, because the yarn is tangled, and it turns out to be a mess instead of a scarf.

"I'll just watch," I say. The guest room upstairs is surrounded with yellow wallpaper. I suppose they are trying something new. I took their eldest daughter's room. Courtney moved to Illinois after she got married to Tom Lennon. I wonder what that is like, with new people, new places. Maybe I should convince Abel to move there, instead.

"Leave me alone, Sadie!" She comes in without my permission. Sadie wearing her bedtime outfit. I usually just wear shorts and a bland shirt. "Here, Daddy's old pair of shoes."

"Eww, those are for old people." They're a pair of tasteless, brown leather shoes.

She skips over, humming, then shuts my window. "La la la la, goodnight."

I wave at her goodnight. I fluff my pillow then close my eyes.

It's been a long time since I had breakfast cooked by someone else. I hear the sizzling, popping sound from the pan as she makes eggs and bacon. Grease is attacking Aunty.

"Where's Uncle Sam?" I say.

"Did you forget CJ is coming? Oh, don't tell me...your father, Corjo! Go clean your face. I still see crust on your eyes. And change into something nice." I completely forgotten they call him CJ.

The food looks mesmerizing, like something you'd find in a popular restaurant. Sadly, she is well-equipped on presentation, but the flavor is . . . yup—tasteless! She knows, but keeps at it anyway.

"Delicious, Mommy!" The young one is wearing a solid white dress and a bow in her hair. I decide to wear a solid black shirt and blue jeans.

"Young lady, what did I say about lying?" She half smiles at her daughter. This is why I always brought Milo over. He gave her exceptional ratings.

"Looks like they are here," Aunty says as I swivel my neck.

My chair skids on the floor, making a sharp irritating noise. Through the window, two figures appear.

"CJ! Uncle!" they both cry out, hugging him.

I give a firm handshake greeting with only a little eye contact. Father has a deep cut probably three inches deep on the side of his face.

"Now brother, what happened to you?"

Father stutters. "I d-d-drunk too much."

Father pats my hair. Every strand he taps makes me want to latch out at him with the same drunken force.

"How you feeling, Pops?"

"Not too bad," he says.

"Would you like some food?" Aunt Lydia asks.

Uncle's head jerks as he sits on the sofa. "No!" he screams. He coughs. "What I meant to say is, maybe later, Lydia dear."

Dad moves his finger toward me, looking at the necklace. He looks at his brother. "She loved that so much."

I shove his hand away. "Sadie, want to play upstairs?" I ask.

Sadie has dolls and a small train set. "You bought marbles like I asked." I say. Her room is a very tight space that only fits two people. A brown carpet in the middle of her floor holds her toys until she is ready for them.

"That's not how you play dolls, Corjo. You will break her. She is my favorite—the rebel, Sarah."

"How do you know? Maybe you have been doing it wrong all along. I want to call her Morgan. Hey! Give her back."

She tucks the doll underneath her feet and turns her back to me. She tilts her neck.

"Not until you learn to play good. I'll get the marbles." She rumbles through her dresser.

I hear marbles rolling in the tin can.

"Just roll them; that's how you play. If I hit all your marbles, you lose. Okay?"

She shakes her head in agreement.

"Hey Sadie, may I talk to my son for a second?" Dad's head peeks through the threshold.

Sadie exits the room, looking back at me.

I wave at her.

"I remember when you bought Carla that necklace. We were so young and in love...and yet, I'm ashamed of my actions these past years. Remember that small house we owned just across the river, with birds waking you up every morning? You wanted to surprise her with a gift after her show."

"Dad, is that why you hate me? Why you took all your pain and dumped it on me?"

Father's breath smells like burnt bacon. "What are you saying, Corjo? I do not hate you. When I said you disgraced me, that was gibberish from anger and my drinking problem."

I grip the train as if I'm choking it. "Mom's death. It's my fault. I remember now, from the moment Uncle placed the necklace in my hand." I take the necklace off. It is warm in my palm.

"My memory is not strong, but when I was younger, I fell off a bridge, right? I dropped it and jumped in after it. How stupid of me." I stare at him. "Say something!"

He sighs. "Mom jumped in after you, but the current was too strong. You were closer to land, so of course, I got you first. That's how she would have wanted it."

"Corjo, I'm sorry. How could I tell you that when you were so young, so attached? You were never separated from her. The necklace you bought for your mother meant so much to you."

"I remember you screaming, 'Wake up, wake up!' and pounding on her chest, but she just kept sleeping. My vibrant mother became so idle, all for this stupid thing. This whole time, I thought she ran from us or was killed but...but..."

"Don't you dare think it's your fault. I alone held that from you, hoping you could sleep well at night. But I was wrong, wasn't I? Every night on the piano, playing her favorite songs . . . it became too much for me, son. Corjo, it drove me insane. I lost faith in everything. I have no excuses but I'll act better, But son every time you played, that day kept ringing in my ears, reminding me of what I lost, my better half. The worst part is, I took it all out on you, my only son."

I place the necklace around his thick neck. He needs it more than me.

"What does one do if the Lord does not hear his prayers? You whisper elsewhere. I cried as your mother lay helplessly in my arms, begging her to breathe once more. Not a second went by without me being reminded of her. I just wanted—"

"To forget? you wanted to forget. All I always wanted is to remember. How selfish of me."

You know, 'a face without a name is intangible, as a name without a face.'"

"What does that mean?" He tries to give back the jewelry, but I refuse it. "What does that mean, son? Here, take this back. She would want you to have it."

I say with a subtle tone, "Nothing, it means nothing."

His silence says it all—he is still bitter.

I would ask him about Abel, but I should believe her. "Guess what, Father? You did good by leaving Alabama. I've met a good friend, a great friend. You hear me? You hear me, Dad?"

I kiss the necklace, then put it around his neck. "I bought this for you, not Mom. She's the one who had the idea, anyway." I leave Sadie's room "Denzel. Son..."

I'm quiet at supper. My other memory of Mom fades, but one still stands clear as the water in my cup. Mommy! Mommy! Why isn't she answering me?

I take a sip of water and the glass ripples. Their voices begin to drown out, then a sudden, sickening pain shoots through my left hand. I excuse myself to go wash my hands, clean the blood and remove the shattered pieces of glass lodged in my palm.

I look in the mirror and don't recognize myself. I start saying my name in my head over and over. It feels weird, like it doesn't fit anymore. I try again. "Corjo. Corjo. Corjo Jones." My tongue twists. I wrap a towel over my left hand. I plummet to the floor, trying to figure out who I am.

My stay with Uncle Sam has come to an end. He escorts us back home. I do not want to go back, but I do want to see her. I even miss her parents. It will be great to see them again. It's been over a month.

"Your piano…you actually did destroy it. Truest of apologies. Corjo, I never meant to mirror my anger at you."

I want to tell him to shut up but choose not to. I take off my uncle's shoes and put them in a bag for Abel's father. I can buy myself another pair and besides, I like it this way better.

The second I open the door to Bell's home, my face encounters her father's fist. If it wasn't for Abel's mother, he would have hit me again.

"Corjo, that you? I'm sorry."

The place is a mess and reeks of a cemetery. It's as if I'm looking at the corpses. They both smell like they haven't bathed. There is shattered glass on the floor.

"I'm okay. I heard you have a new daughter. I would like to meet her."

I wish I hadn't said that because her mother falls to her knees, holding her belly like something is missing. She unfolds the white cloth on her head. She frantically shakes it, shrieking and sobbing.

Moot's body turns away from his love. Moot tells me what happened.

He must be lying, but Ma looks like the awful truth never fled the room. She starts to cough.

"What's wrong?" She holds her face in a sick motion.

"She's sick," Moot answers.

"I have to leave, but I'll come back The following day I go back and take some medicine with me.

She grazes my nose and Abel's father expresses his gratitude with a thank you. Both adults act like complete strangers. Moot's eyes itch to look at his wife. I don't understand. Moot looks like he is ready for sleep, ready for the next day to come, even though its morning. Her smile is forever gone. She looks like she never stopped crying.

Engulfed in rage, I feel my lip bleeding. Their garden is dead outside. Ma just sits still. Her hand moves back and forth on the sofa, not even looking but staring with no purpose at the fireplace. Both eyes are dried of tears. I know she doesn't normally say much, but this is different.

To Abel. I came over after I returned from my uncle's. The nearest hospital was by his house and that was where I stayed. You have to know I did want to come sooner.

I picked up the letter that Bell had left and saw it was open. Your parents told me what happened, and Abel, they looked devastated. Your mom, her eyes were filled with sorrow but your dad…Abel, I don't know what to make of him. He saw the gates of Hades. They're the same eyes my father carries. My father made a full recovery. I wanted to add that as well, maybe you will rest easy after hearing that.

Your dad came at me like I was to blame. I see how you feel when someone judges you just because you wear the opposite hue. I was scared at first, but he calmed down when he recognized it was me, thanks to your mother. If I had been any other person, I would fear for their life. They wanted to know what the letter held so I read it to them. Margo had a lot to say.

Dear Abel,

If you are reading this, it means I was too much of a coward, but believe me, I tried. I hope you can forgive me. I beg you, please don't stay at the house when I'm gone. A man named Braxton will probably come. If you ever hear this name, run! He will stop at nothing to bring your father or the whole family into slavery. I kept him at bay for all these years, hoping to atone for ever letting myself follow after him. I was young and foolish. I only wish I had someone to help me as your mother and father do for you.

My husband, Braxton, works with a colleague from time to time. I've witnessed this man work and, deary, it's horrendous. What he does, he shreds families to pieces and doesn't even break a sweat nor raise a brow. He goes by many names but the one that sticks the most is Harvest. I knew I had to run off with my son and your father. I don't want you to go through that at all, be another part of his job. A piece to sacrifice. I don't want you to be another chapter in his conquest. I love you and your father and hope your Ma is doing well. She talked about a child once, well, you know what I mean. I know that kid will be in great hands. Hopefully another daughter. I can't wait! If I'm not around by then, give her my best regard. Make sure you read to her, but I know you already will.

I was suffering from Diphtheria, which caused me to have shortness of breath, swelling, and my muscles became feeble. I could barely stand at times. I never told you because I did not want to burden you with my own plight. I wanted you to be literate, but I suppose your mom had a hand in that. She wanted your life to be different, so she asked me. How could I refuse such a loving woman? To tell you the truth, I copied her short hairstyle as my own. I think she noticed and it made us a lot closer. I remember how she asked, she came up to me, picked a book and papers, and at that moment, I already knew. Also, I left enough food for you guys where only you will find it. Times are harder and with a baby on the way, it's the least I could do.

I want you to know that I'm forever grateful that you came into my life, the daughter I always wanted. I am so proud of you! I know I was tough on you, but it was only to help you prosper into the beautiful and intelligent woman I know you are meant to be. Never did I mean to hurt you when you were younger, but you were hard to deal with—never could stay focused on your lessons until I started scolding. Don't worry, I don't dislike you for misbehaving. It's okay, you can laugh. I never was funny, was I? You were the spice of my life. It must be hard for you to read this.

By the way, this is how you spell writer and Abel. Silent letters, right? I never was a fan either, but as you read this, I suppose I became silent as well. I pray Flint gives this to you! Trust me, he won't read this. That boy is dumber than the pig we had when you were five. Well deary, I hope all is well and always know I cherish our moments. You are an unstoppable force. Keep on reading. I'd love to read your book one day. You know my name and have seen my face, so what does that leave you? Someone that loves you and you will remember, I pray. Bye deary.

I read it to Moot and your mother. How should I feel? I lost you like a wildfire came by and left everything in ashes, but that would be a pleasant way to put it. It still burns and scorches my heart.

If we are feeling like this, I cannot imagine what you're going through. I took up prayers. Maybe just once the Lord will open his ears. I'm done whispering elsewhere. You taught me that. I'll change, welcome the good Lord. Just come home safe. I also have done a lot of studying. Maybe you can tell. Let's play chess soon, okay? I forget who's ahead.

I'll check on your folks whenever I get the chance. I'll be traveling back and forth, but I swear I'll see them again.

Hi Abel, I'm writing to you once again. I came back another three months later. Sorry, I have been on the move, but my house on Gazel Road is still there if you ever want to stay. Just make sure you wipe your feet.

I don't think you want to hear this, but your parents don't say as much to each other as I have witnessed in the past. They used to engage in lively conversations that had love in their voice and action. Your father became violently ill again. He started coughing and is looking brittle. I brought him more medicine. He made a good recovery and Mama too.

# Chapter 14



I'm living my life as a slave to the Meade family. They live on the coast side of Virginia on a plantation that stretches far and wide. The man who purchased me goes by the name of Dante, also known as Dante the Inferno. He has a beautiful wife, April, and two children. Massa is having a party. He invites all his important friends, or at least they sure act as if they were all senators or mayors.

Ice clinks inside their glasses as they order more wine or water, swirling their cups filled with red liquid.

"Yes, Massa," I say and pour more. Massa has cherry red hair, a broad face, and eyes that are green like summer grass.

The rooks mock him when we are alone. He has a scar across his nose. Aunty calls him woodpecker because of his long nose. It reminds me of the raven's beak I saw long ago while sitting with Corjo.

We prepare hot bread and butter with wedges of cheese. They are devouring white chicken breast. There was a request, more like a demand, to remove the skin. The aroma lingers in the air. Pumpkin pie for a sweet aftertaste.

The room is nicely lit with an oil lamp in the center. Dangling like stars is a golden chandelier with almost ten candles in its holder. Their table sits on a brown rug with intricate dark swirls along the borders. There is a rack for drinks on the right side of the white walls. Next to it is an empty shelf with loose papers. Above is a painting.

Dante entertains his guests with jokes as he sits at the head of the table. His wife, April, is to the left. I'm careful not to drop the bottle or overfill their glass. Massa is never happy when we act "a fool," as he says.

He shouts, "If you look like a fool, imagine how I feel around my company." His face is rosy afterwards.

April points at her empty cup and I rush over. "More, Abel. Chop, chop." She taps on the glass with her silverware. It rings like a bell. Her voice is sweet like flowers. She has long blonde hair. April is in a blue cutaway gown, with a draped overskirt. A blue crystal hang around her thin bony neck. The other women are equally as beautiful. The two dark-haired women are wearing black and blue blouses. Her friend to the left of April eats with gloves. Her husband, is equally as weird. I stare at him for quite some time. He licks the chicken breast before eating it.

The other servants are passing out dishes or preparing more food. We all look alike, wearing puffy, purple dresses with white aprons. The guests stay for hours, which means the young boys cannot leave until they are satisfied. The young boys dress in blue vests and gray wool trousers. It's the only time they look well groomed.

His buddies always stroke his ego. "I love how your slaves are tamed, Dante."

Another one adds, "The new title suits you. There is fire underneath that gut."

Dante the Inferno nods at his accomplished work. I became what they might call a house nigger but that's not my only role. On Fridays and Saturdays, I'm out picking cotton like the rest or teaching their child. Ironically, Margo was right.

I overhear Massa saying his ranch is six hundred acres. I don't know the exact size, but grass and trees are all around and white balls stretch around his home.

I've come to know and respect the women that guide me. We became friends through false grace. I shouldn't say this, but if I knew my life would turn this way, I would wish to come here earlier.

My friend liked to be called "Aunty," so we called her that. However, her full name was Antebellum. She had no last name. Aunty was not as lucky as I am. I miss her so much.

There are at least thirty of us working. A couple of us are inside the house and the rest are always in the heat, slaving. There is a constant struggle to make weight. If they don't make their demand, they receive lashes. They tie their arms on a post and swing away, each whip biting at their flesh.

His oldest child, Monta Meade, is the most dangerous, always itching to beat one of us even if we never cause trouble—just to keep us in check. It's been too long since I last tasted the snake bite. It makes you plead for forgiveness but what's there to beg about? No one attempts to run. They have given up, and I am scared too. The rooks talk about going North if they were ever to run but it's a false dream. Massa's son and the overseer make sure. Nobody wants to have the same fate as the ones they do find.

Dante delivers a speech that would warm your heart. He reminds us that we are part of his luscious family. He expresses, "If one of my own goes missing, I will take all the necessary measures to bring them back where they belong: dogs, bounty hunters, and all the resources at my disposal. After all, we are a family. We take care of our own." He reminds us that we are his family in the dirtiest way. Dante continues, "This is your home. Treat it with respect and don't ever test my patience."

"Yes, Massa," we say.

Inside, his home sparkles from the Meade's black and blue square tile floor. The bottom half of the wall is painted blue and the top half is white. There are many alluring crystals hanging from the ceiling with candles. Below the crystals is a circular red rug in the center. There are several bookshelves and cabinets and desks with fine plates set on top spread across the big house. There is a grandfather clock on the inside wall right by the door. Above the clock is an oval mirror. Next to the clock, on the other side of the door, is a black potted baby tree. It rests in front of a window.

The items that stand out the most are the black pianos they own. One is upstairs in the Misses' private area and another downstairs.

I hate to admit it, but one thing that kept me close to my parents is gone—shoes are now attached to my feet. They have all the house slaves in uniforms. The day Massa welcomed me into his home, he made me change my style. More accurately, his wife presented me with a gift.

They whipped at my feet until I couldn't disobey any longer. I stood still. If I were to hop around, the overseer became angrier and fiercer. The lash of the whip cracked the air. But that pain is nothing compared to what I committed and what I've seen. You have to believe me, I only sought out what I thought was best for my sister. I suppose I should state where Ina is. After all, I took on the role of her mother, though it may be a lie.

# Chapter 15

Ladder year of 1859

My worth as a human is five hundred eighteen. Just like many families were separated from each other, Meade is trying to take my sister away from me. Is it intentional? Probably not, but does he care? Do they even consider how we feel?

I am about to get hauled away, Ina still in my arms. I squirm like a mad woman on the platform. Blood drips from my mouth but there is no way I'm letting go. "She bit me."

The people in charge beat me.

A familiar face stands up for me. "This monster is trying to separate a mother from her child! Sir, if you continue down this road, I will be forced to write about your plantation and expose it in the New York Tribune," Henry Doe shouts to Meade and the crowd. I'm looking like a lost animal in the woods. The only option I have is to pray someone can assist with my struggles.

"You wouldn't dare. Nothing states that what I'm doing is illegal. Why should I heed your futile warning?" Dante fires back with insensitive words.

"I know it's your right as an owner, but you don't need this kind of heat against you. Think about it. If I wanted, I could shut down your whole business without batting an eye."

My owner grunts and moans. His expression goes from understanding to frustration.

Dante puts his hands out, "No thank you. I came a long way. You don't scare me. I only want a few slaves and nothing more."

They escort me off the platform, my hands chained. I feel my voice growing faint. I'm fighting gravity before I lose her. I drop my whole body weight to the ground. The chains make a loud noise. That does not slow them. "Ina! Ina!" I look like other families. Why would I receive any special treatment? I join the four other slaves Meade bought. We are leaving Savannah.

I see Doe chasing behind us. "Stop!" I see my sister held in front of the horses. They gallop in place before trampling him. "I bought her myself, so please do me the honor and take her, she is nothing but an infant. Have a soul."

My owner glares at me with utter irritation, "This your child, girl? Because if it's not—"

I nod ferociously, "Yes sir. Yes, yes." He takes his hat and waves, allowing Ina on board. "AHHH," I cried and cried. "Thank you. Thank you."

Henry Doe walks away, winks my way, then brings his hat down on his golden hair, covering his blessed blue eyes. I look at that man with the compassion that I show Pa and Ma—nothing but admiration, love, and, above all, gratefulness. I hold Ina like she is my own. I hold her tight and never let go.

"Hyahh," Dante says. We are headed to his farm, located in Virginia.

We arrive and that's when he gives his family speech. He introduces us to himself and his land. His white family comes out. "Good afternoon. I'm April. This is Monta and my baby, Ariana."

Dante tells us we have to pick cotton first thing tomorrow morning, so we'd better get plenty of rest.

# Chapter 16

I am alone with Ina in an enclosed shed on a small mattress.

"Hello. I'm Antebellum, but they calls me Aunty."

I just look at her. In another scenario, I probably would have hidden behind Ma's legs, exactly how I did when I was younger.

"I gets it, child. It ain't fair. Lawd knows yous young. Everyone real nice, you ought to meet em." She has a really thick voice. She makes Ma and Pa sound white. I notice the difference right away.

She grips my hand and forces me toward the noisy crowd. Ina is asleep, so my body moves on its own. Aunty has a white cloth wrapped on her head like Mama. Her shoes and dress are worn out. She is a small thin woman with dark brown eyes.

"Everyone, this here is...ahh...uhm," she whispers to me, "what they call you?"

"Abel," I respond.

"Apple!" Her face swells with a smile.

"Abel," I repeat, slightly upset.

"That be what I say, Apple. She joins us in tonight's game, or at least watch. This is my shed by the way."

They all say hi and welcome me. The men are in brown or tan trousers that come to their knees or their ankles. The women's gowns are of the same color and made of the same material, cotton. Only two are present in Aunty's shack and they have head wraps. Both have no shoes.

Aunty explains the game and tells me I can help her. The game is called Ludo and it looks like it is played by four. They have a big square paper with small and large squares drawn all around, with blue, yellow, green, and red on each corner, and a center square which is home base.

"Abel, all yous gotta do is get your piece from your start to finish."

It looks so fun when they are playing. It's a simple game, really. They roll the dice to get a chance around the board. However, you have to roll a six first, before you can move out your home base. It gets tricky when everyone has their pieces out.

They keep yelling, "Eat it, eat her! Eat him!"

I ask Aunty what the commotion is about.

"Oh child, eat it. Take they color token. Whenever yous roll a dice and land on a square they on, that piece yours now. Like that! Now, Bo my worker."

Bo is in a faded blue shirt and brown pants like the others but he is a sturdy fellow. His nose is impressively big.

I watch them play Ludo for quite some time. Aunty explains more.

When Bo's turn comes up, he rolls a three but instead of him moving his piece, Aunty moves her red piece. Bo has to toss a six and that is his only way to get out from under Aunty's clutches. Players have a second option—use that same six to bring out your color piece and become free. It's all about strategy and a bit of luck.

Whenever you choose to get your color token from their jail, it appears you have to start over from your safe zone even if you were at the endpoint. There are a total of four pieces required to make it home. The first one done with getting all four pieces safely around is the winner.

"Lawd, get my chillens home. Hand me the glass! Five!" a woman says. I understand her better than Aunty. The dice hitting the glass makes a soft sound. They use glass, so the dice can roll better.

The game is intense. Everyone is yelling, "Four, four. Eat her, eat her back, Bo!"

Sadly, couple turns later Bo is unlucky. He hits a five, which means he's now one space in front of Malcolm.

Malcolm is the other name I manage to remember. His hair is nappy, and his voice is bittersweet. He is one of the few wearing shoes and they are in fine shape.

"Blow here, child," Aunty says.

I do as she ask, puckering my lips and blowing out hot air.

"One!"

Everyone is laughing as Bo is eaten once again. The small shed shakes from being overcrowded. There are three people on the mattress. Four more surround the board on the cool ground. I kneel down beside Aunty.

Bo is in last place. He still has three pieces while everyone else is down to two. Bo scratches his bald head.

"How do you win?" I ask.

The room is thick with heat. No one is sitting down on Aunty's chair. It smells a bit bitter but not foul like the cell in Georgia.

The last rule is, in order to win, you have to roll the right numbers to finish. It's six spaces to finish and, say you were in the fifth, only a one on the dice would win; any other roll makes you wait until your next turn.

"Keep the door open," someone on the mattress says. He has a deep voice.

The night is fun. Never did I imagine I would meet these people. They are all complete strangers but act like they have known each other since birth. They use a pine torch for lighting.

I think Bo cheated because he is the winner. Everyone is speechless. It's hilarious. Bo finally ate a piece of the yellow player, and his pieces sprinted home before anyone else did.

They scatter after the long-lasting Ludo game. It's nothing like chess, but both games have their own excitement. Bo is mocking everyone for doubting him. He is a lovely fellow, but his rough voice doesn't help his case nor do the gaping scars on his hands.

"Whateva. Quiet, Bo."

"Come here, Apple."

I won't bother trying to correct her. I follow her, and we sit underneath a big depressed-looking tree. The leaves and branches hang down like it's weeping.

"Look here, child. Tomorrow, I want you to stay away from Jonathan. He go 'bout like he be in charge, swinging his whip carelessly. Have an eye for him, you best mind yourself." She stares at me for some time. "You not fooling no one. That ain't your baby. Don't worry, none my bidness. Won't say none."

"The master would have sold my baby elsewhere if I said anything else. How did you know?"

In her heavy accent, she says, "Look at you—yous a twig. Your hips not much for motherhood. Not yet." She takes a deep breath. "When tomorrow comes, beg mistress to take care of that child. She good in the shed for now, but no place for her."

I stare at Aunty.

"Bo. He seems more than a stranger to you."

She blushes and nervously laughs. "Oh, he be my husband. Kind man."

I'm not surprised. Seeing how they looked at each other while playing reminded me of Pa and Mama.

"We have a boy, he ten. Massa have him in the house fanning, but he also in the fields passing out water at times."

She grits her teeth. "I hate him." Her facade shifts like the tree above us, with a dash of anger.

"Who?"

"Jonathan. Laid hands on my baby, my boy. All I could do was watch!"

I am ready to ask the next question, but she reads my mind.

"Cliff."

We return to my shed. I feed Ina food and Aunty shows me the proper way to change her and place her into clothes that fit cleanly.

Ma never did get a chance to share her outfits with Ina, but I'm keeping an open mind that someday we will be reunited. Someday, this nightmare will end. If it doesn't, I will run with my sister. I'll do what Ma did and just keep running.

Aunty leaves. The mattress is covered with a miserable blanket and pillow. I don't own much so my shack is pretty empty. There is one small window with a tattered pink cloth. Broken and whole jars are scattered on the floor or set on a miserable lonely shelf. My floor is filled with dirt even though an ill-looking broom stands in the corner. Some shacks have chimneys but this one does not. Ina glares at the door, waiting for Mama or Papa to barge in, I imagine.

I sit down and wrap my arms around her. She smells nice but nothing like Mama or Papa anymore.

We both look at the door. "I miss them too."

# Chapter 17

They line us up in the wee morning hours. The sun hasn't even woken up.

There are at least twenty of us. Everyone is in the same rags.

"For the new guys, I'm Jonathan and to my right is Redd." They gallop back and forth on their horses. Jonathan has a rash on the lighter part of his right arm. He has thick brown hair. Jonathan is a chunky, short man. I can tell he is short. Compared to Redd, he barely reaches the horse's straps.

Redd is mysteriously quiet, just waiting for one of us to fail. There is a small mole below his right nostril. His hat is tied around his neck. His chin is chiseled, fitting his burly figure, and his eyes are light blue.

"Today is Monday. You rooks will pick cotton. For those that are new, two-hundred pounds will be your weight to meet. Fail and..." He points at Redd, his whip dangling like the horse's tail. He frightens me. They both do.

The morning's delicate breeze is cool. I remember Aunty telling me to always drink water. I have an old, brown, tattered sack; it almost appears like the cotton may fall through. I take a drink out of a bucket right after someone else. I draw water with a large spoon. Some water spills, so I wipe my hands across my face then dab it on my dress.

The sun swells up. I'm happy Ina is too young to be out here. I lose count after thirty-five, but I keep driving myself. Fresh water comes by in the hands of both boys and girls. My palms are sweaty and annoyingly sticky.

My hand burns and it stings. When I take a drink for the second time, it's like a fresh stream gushing down from a waterfall, refreshing. My tongue welcomes it.

"Are you Cliff?" I ask a young boy.

He shakes his head "no" and points his bony finger at the big house. He's in trousers that are bigger than him. The boy holds his trousers with his hands. His neck is thin with a small gut. His eyes are exhausted, and he has no hair.

I suppose I will get the honor of meeting Cliff another time.

"Stop talking!" Jonathan jumps off his white horse. He whips at my feet then at the bucket. He wastes more than water. Jonathan spills our life supply.

"No more!" shouts Jonathan.

The slaves stop working and try to scoop the water on the ground. To my surprise, they swallow the mud whole then hurl it out. The water is lost in the soil. It's awful. I feel like it's my fault.

"Sorry," I softly whisper.

Their knuckles are firm with rage and their backs damp with sweat. I hear mumbling and cussing. Walking around, I feel chilled. I dig my head into my shoulders. I hope no one hates me.

I see Aunty and Bo hastily working.

My back is stressed from bending. The air is warm and smells of dried sweat. The foreheads of the others are shiny. They don't bother wiping the sweat away.

Jonathan and Redd are doing their sweeps. The lack of water makes me feel faint. My mouth is so dry, it hurts to swallow. It's like eating dry grains.

The sun is beating intensely on my chest, back, and neck. I keep picking one piece of cotton at a time. I fan my fingers to provide my own breeze since the wind has decided to take a day off. I would like to join it.

"Line up!" His voice is rough.

Water is waiting at the end once they weigh us. Aunty is far on the other side, so I can't talk to her. I grip my sack with a calm mindset.

"Go get yourself a drink, next," Jonathan says. Redd stands at his left.

The workers gulp the water violently, with passion. Malcolm is not far behind me. His face makes me squirm every time I look.

"You, come."

It's almost my turn. I grip the sack tight. The brown, gloomy bucket brims with gold and riches. The idea of massacring the water is all I'm thinking about. Spit, I thought dried, reappears, my lips ashier than my knees. I'm eager for a divine drink. Two more people. I'm behind two elderly women, maybe older than Margo. The backs of their elbows hang with loose flesh.

"Your turn."

I hadn't noticed, but he has a pick in his teeth. Redd hurls out a chunky piece of spit. Bo and Aunty are taking their drinks.

"Stop." The water barely touches my lips, only one pitiful drop. My tongue and teeth attack each other for moisture. I bite my lips before I allow that drop to slip. Redd strikes the spoon. I plummet to the ground trying to scoop what's left. Mud never tasted so good. I find myself sucking the liquid, pretty much eating dirt.

"You useless garbage. You couldn't even make two hundred and that's low."

"What! No, I did make it. Count again, please," I say. They do and it's the same result. "One hundred sixty-three pounds."

Jonathan says, "Redd, you know what to do. Make sure this rook learns."

Redd yanks at my arms. "Up."

My body is tugged from the earth.

Just a sip.

Redd escorts me away from the others. "Ten lashes. Next time, I add five. Understand?" Redd says calmly.

I hear him take a huge breath, one that expresses this is going to tire me. There is a post on the right side of the house further down from the sad tree.

One lash. The pain is easily noticed. Two lashes. I begin to scream. I bite my top lip. Three. More gut-wrenching sounds spill from my lips. I cry. Four hits.

I'm pleading for mercy, "Stop I beg you! Stop."

Five. I'm at a dark place, just incapable of forgiving. Crying, shrieking with fear and panic. Six.

"Ahhhh! Stop, please! I feel like I might die."

Seven. My mind goes blank. More blood spills from my back. Eight. How many times did Ma and Pa endure the venomous snake bites? Nine. Who am I to you? Ten. Ina. I'll do whatever it takes to keep you from this.

Redd leaves and I'm on the ground, throbbing in agonizing torment like nothing I've experienced. I wouldn't even wish this on Flint, better yet, Braxton. My back is like a washboard.

"Clean her up. Make sure she is ready for tomorrow!" Redd says. He walks inside.

My mouth tastes of blood. My arms are tied around the log post and my clothing is ripped.

"Abel. Abel?"

Someone begins to untie me.

My eyes are blurry, and my wrists are bruised.

"I'm so sorry I should've–"

I cut Aunty off. My voice has no hate nor joy, but nothing comes out. My back stings like hundred of stabs from a pin. My clothes are tattered with claw marks, they disgustingly attach to my back. The warmness of my blood streams down my thighs, making me want to jump out of my skin with no desire to return.

Aunty and another woman grab me and run to a shack. They lay me on my stomach.

I desperately crave to retaliate, tie them down to experience the same torment. Give them a taste before they tear my flesh, before unnecessary blood trickles.

"Softer," I whine, still crying. They are efficient at cleaning my wounds, like it's an everyday occurrence. What if every day is like this?

"Hold still, child. This will sting now," Aunty says. A refreshing liquid oozes down my back with a jolt of lighting.

"What is that?" I shout. The pain burns for a second then descends.

"Best you don't know." Antebellum holds me down tight.

The mattress shakes as my body trembles. I bite down into the cloth they gave me. I feel more dabs from a towel. My legs kick with shock. The air smells sour but I think I like it. The shack is full of supplies. I see a whole supply of towels and blankets.

Food is served on a table in front of Dante's home. The ladies that cook in the bigger shacks outside make okra, some chicken, more meat, and many other delights. They eat with their hands, grabbing a big portion of their meal. I only grab a cup of water. If I eat the food, it will only make me vomit. I stumble away, exerting a hissing noise, as my back aches.

Night comes. My stomach is not happy with me and attacks from the inside. "Here, eat up. You gonna need your strength." Aunty and Bo both have food for me.

She also feeds Ina. "This my fight, Bo," I hear her say.

Bo adds, "Morrow, I's add some to her bag, try to help best we can."

"Abel, make sure you give Massa the child."

I do not say anything.

They leave shortly after Ina and I eat.

The night is ending. I can't sleep, only tossing from my stomach to my sides, avoiding my back. It was an awful day. The pain is indescribable. I smell of dried sweat.

Ina is beginning to reek. It's hard to wipe her bottom. The smell is so sharp it attacks me before I can defend myself. I should bathe her soon. I pray tomorrow is not a repeat of today.

Day two, I get off easy. I stay in my shack with Ina, but I'm too tired to move. Ina is still sleeping.

I hear the overseers shouting from outside. My body is tightly wrapped in a tan cloth.

The next day, I'm forced back to picking cotton. My back has yet to recover, but I manage. I know they don't care.

I continue moving the cotton into my bag. I'm faster than yesterday. There is plenty of water spread around. The young men and women are hard at work, keeping us quenched. It helps with the sweat and heat.

"Cliff. Cliff!" a man and woman holler. The boy rushes over to them. "Thank you."

Redd is glaring at me, anticipating my failure, once again. I mind my business.

The cotton bolls are soft. I repeat to myself. Pull the boll and drop the cotton in my sack. Leave the stalk behind. Come on, Abel. Faster. Faster. My legs and arms move quickly. The fewer water breaks I take, the better. I repeat, pull the boll and drop the cotton in my sack. My sides ache. I take a deep breath.

I overhear two adults talking. I think one woman's name is Lonny, but I'm not sure about her friend.

"Did you hear what Massa son done again?" Lonny whispers. "That boy ain't right, Georgia."

"I know. He even lashes at the kids. Look here." She rolls her sleeves up, showing whip scars that dried and healed nastily. "I know. Weren't none my children neither. But you know we all family."

"Was it my boy again? He stubborn. I pray weren't my daughter. Poor child too young to know what she be. They all are."

"Line up," Jonathan says.

Aunty and Bo run toward me. They quietly shove in some cotton, making my sack feel slightly heavier. Three are behind me.

"What you got this time?" Jonathan gives a cocky snarl. "Two hundred thirteen." Jonathan fidgets, then passes me. A relieved sigh surfaces.

Day and night, the same routine—more picking, then supper time.

Monta and Redd are in charge. He is a slender man, shorter than his father, but a close copy, with the same fire red hair and the same high cheekbones.

"Line up!" Monta is in charge today, which is Friday. His voice is filled with anger. Both of his hands are folded behind his back. I'm next.

Redd is to the right of him. His posture is elegant and calm.

"One hundred."

"Liar! You sinful man!" Aunty screams.

Monta ignores her. "Redd, add five more this time, right?"

He nods. "I'll take this one. Cannot have you hog all the fun."

My head is shaking frantically. I know it's a mistake.

He even allows me to drink.

"Sir, why?" I desperately ask. He shoves me while Redd attends to the others.

"Let's go," Monta says. His green eyes drown me with fear.

My breath is gone. I'm looking around like a blind man.

"Let's go," he repeats.

I can't move. My back still throbs but my heart pulses even faster.

Redd practically drags me over to the log post, then ties me. He takes the whip coil by his hip.

One. Ina? Two. Ina. Three. Ina. Four. Ina. Five. Ina! Six. Ma, I . . . I understand.

Dante is standing there, watching. "Monta, that's enough! I paid good money. Don't kill her."

"But, Father..." His voice is bitter.

My back surges with devilish pain. Blood is dripping down my torn shirt.

"I said, enough!"

Monta hurls the whip down and heads back to the underworld, not even breaking a sweat but everything is broken in me. He doesn't untie me. He whispers, "Run, and it's the last mistake you make."

Fear shakes my legs.

Again, I'm rendered useless. Again, I feel discomfort that laughs with a stifling strike.

The slaves are eating. It's a little past midday. I get up after another cleaning by Aunty. I do not join but only move to visit my sister. My mind is fixed on a solid thought.

Ina is awake, awaiting my return. I grab her. Tears flow down my cheeks, dripping on her face. Her soft hand extends to my cheeks.

I take my younger sister to the bathhouse to clean her up. No one is around. She looks so excited to see me. I feel the same emotion. The tub is already filled but it's not dirty. I chime a word to her. Ina makes some gibberish noise. The bathhouse is small. The tub is in the center. The window is boarded shut. It smells nice. I see jars of liquid soap.

"I won't let anything happen to you." I mean it, but I think this is the only option. I drop her in the tub and kiss her on the forehead. Bubbles rise and pop to the surface but soon enough...no more.

# Chapter 18

Footsteps stampede toward me and a sharp pain radiates from my left cheek.

"What you thinkin?" Ina is pulled out from the belly of the tub by Bo.

Aunty's face is confused, angry, yet empathetic. "They done taint your mind child! Why would you?"

I feel like I am coming out of a deep, uncontrolled sleep.

"I think she coming to, Antebellum." Bo is helping Ina. I see him pressing rapidly against her chest. I hear her crying as she resurrects.

My body quakes with doubt. My hands are stained with an odor that won't wash off. "I'm so sorry! I...I thought..."

Aunty slowly walks up to me. Her hand is high up.

I wince for a moment but instead, she hugs me.

"Precious Abel." I cry even harder.

"I'm a terrible sister. I tried to kill my own family. I'm a monster!" I'm in tears. My chest is swollen with more pain than the whip could ever muster.

"Believe me, child, they change all us. They turn us into monsters, make you do unspeakable acts." She hugs me tighter. Her body warm.

I drop to my knees, trying to shove her off but she holds on.

Bo brings Ina over. She is soaking wet and coughing. Ina locks eyes with me. It's like her beacon of light disappeared. She couldn't see through the thick fog and neither could I.

"Aunty, my sister...she just kept looking at me, praying I would reach in to grab her. All I did was look away. Ah! I looked away, Aunty and I—"

"Shhh, shhh, shhhh." Her eyes are red as well, but she finds the strength to hold me.

"Abel, can I tell you a story?"

My head is buried deep in her chest. Ina's screams and my sobs nearly surpass her voice. Sorrow doesn't even come close to how I feel. How can I even call myself family?

"If yous think you a monster, I guess that's why Cliff will never forgive me. How could he? I be the worst mum around."

"Antebellum, don't," Bo says softly but his rough voice makes it sound more aggressive than calm.

"It's time I share my secrets and allow the roots to birth me anew. The one that been carving into my soul for long."

"Inaaaa!" I keep shouting. I can't calm down. "If I said I wanted to take my own life, it wouldn't even come close to the spear I just cast, the darkness that is devouring her, me." I shut my eyes close. My heart is heavy.

"Abel, forgive yourself!" Bo says. "Your sister, she gots enough heart for both of yous. I mean just look at her."

I do. She wants me.

"I don't deserve her."

Bo, Aunty, my sister, and I are on the dirt floor. Bo rubs the back of his darling,

"Go ahead." Bo tries to hand me Ina, but I refuse his gesture. I can't do it. That privilege has retired. Aunty looks down at me, my head press deep in her dress.

"Not too long ago…I wish that it never happened but child, it did. Cliff was our first child. We had one more on its way. She be a beautiful one. She not born yet, but I knew. The thought of her living this inhumane life like her parents and brother was not gonna happen. I told Bo and Cliff we were going to escape. My boy, he smart. He be the only person to say no, let's not. Me being hard-headed, I didn't listen. They say follow the drinking gourd till you hit a river, then keep running until Northern states are at eye.

"Abel, everything is all right. Your sister fine. Don't shed anymore tears. But, we didn't tell anyone, just the four us will be gone. My plan was simple—run after a day of slaving done right. At supper time, fill our bellies. When everyone around, they wouldn't notice our disappearance. I also waited after the two-week headcount Massa give."

I feel tears hitting my scalp. She is hurting. I might as well be looking in a reflecting glass. Her voice grows softer.

"Abel, if only I listened. We were on the run. Everything was looking great. The night guided us. These raggedy colorless clothes we wear day in and out did not pose no trouble neither. We stole the brown sacks to store some food for us. Anyways, we kept going but soon daybreak came. My boy became hungry, upset, and tired. Not much food. I gave him what we had. Bo eating as well. They ask if I ate.

"Lucky for us, through the woods, we find a broken wagon. We let the night pass us as we stay nice and cool, surrounded by owls and rustling leaves. The air is both thick and fragile. We constantly looking over our shoulders.

"Day and night came and gone. I sat down on a log and watch them eat and drink the last of our rations. Abel, it must have been three, maybe four days. I don't know, we lost count. Like Massa says, we family. The slave catcher were hot on us. I became real weak and couldn't continue. Bo carried me for the most part. I felt like I was holding them back. My belly heavy. We crossed many a river, covering ourselves in dirt so no hounds can trace us. It was a scary time, a time of survival. My boy was so scared. He didn't know how to swim. Bo carrying all three of us, through the depth of the cold river. I know he had to be tired, but this man saw a light I didn't see. He kept going for our sake. We almost hit a Northern state. I believe it be Ohio, maybe.

"Yous know what, it wasn't even the worse part to see freedom stripped from us once more. My nightmare just began when I saw his poor little eyes forever shut down. I couldn't even rewind his clock. Cliff didn't see himself as a slave as we do. Abel, you ask how can you forgive yourself. Let me ask you something. How can I forgive my own self, how can he?

"Back on the plantation, Dante surprisingly show us mercy. I thought it be a blessing from the good lawd. It wasn't till later that I found out Cliff and Bo absorb my punishment. Jonathan and Monta happily done they part. Lashes everywhere, they bodies were like roots coming out a tree. They took my lashes my poor boys, my boys! And what I give them in return, more ways than I could imagine, strip them of their happiness."

"It was time for the baby to be born. I told my boy he gets to name his kid brother or sister. My boy expression looks like it all been worth once he seen his sibling, the misery of the lash gone."

"Antebellum, that's enough. You don't have to."

She continues. Her voice is fragile, her breathing stifled. Her grip tightens. "Cliff face lit up as his kinfolk was about to get delivered. 'Mama, Papa, can we call him Nemo? I just know he will be a boy, my brother.' He excited. Nemo a fine name, I tells him. We all was happy. I remember how tight Bo held my palm. I couldn't tell if he or me was the one sweating. I looks at both of them. 'Maybe Juju for a girl, always did want a baby sister too,' Cliff said. I may have screamed but his laugh ease the pain of birth focus on him none else. His soft smile more of a remedy then any ol' herbs."

"What happened, Aunty?" My voice is muffled, still pressed in her chest. I hear Ina and Bo's heavy breaths and her soft sob. I feel a bit anxious.

"Abel, during my whole run I didn't eat for those days. Believe me, I felt fine. I wanted to be the strong mama for my boys. There wasn't much food left. Was it selfish of me? The wet nurse, Fannie, helps bring my baby into the world. Her face turn sour. Fannie said she wasn't making a noise. When Cliff looked at me, the flicker of hope just went out right in front of me. Those nights when you cannot see the stars. I think I done stole all that 'way. There was emptiness. I felt Bo palm. It was moist but cold, slowly, painfully letting go. He walks to the corner and…Abel, that was the worst part of my life. I never seen him cry, not even from whips."

Aunty is talking through her tears. "I don't even care no more, lash me, embarrass me. I rather let my baby live a life of misery than not at all! I was traumatized. My beautiful baby, she didn't make it. I held her motionless body and…and…and…I couldn't get a word."

"It took Bo a long time to forgive me, but Cliff hasn't since."

"You didn't need my forgiveness, Antebellum. Sorry if I makes yous feel that way. I just wanted to hold that child. That what kept me going." He is looking at Ina "that would brought happiness for all. Just like you Ina.

"Thank you. I haven't talked to my boy like a mother should to a son since the day we decides to escape—foolish, unforgivable. It's not a grudge he held but something else, a why? Of course, a young boy won't understand. He thought he was free for all he known. His family is here. He has friends. How could I be free knowing that I took a life, my own?! My actions are beyond my own forgiveness, but you, child…look at your sister. She happy. Show us they can't break you apart. As for me, my boy can't stand to look my way. I might as well color my skin and call my own dam self a cracka, cause that's how he sees me. I know, because that's the glare I give 'em whites."

I look around the room. Both of them are smiling behind all those wrinkles of suffering.

"Child, do you know where the word rook came from?"

"Yes, a little. Pa told me it's to raise self-esteem amongst the Negroes. I forget the rest."

"Yes, that be part to a bigger whole." Aunty scratches her head. "We tired of them changing things, claiming as they own. Rook is a word to show power have a purpose, the beginning and end, just like on a cheese board. We are the foundation that built this nation. We needed hope, write our own history, no more like a different history. You hear?"

"Chess, Aunty."

She hits my head. "Shush now, that be what I say—cheese." The tears on her face have dried. My face is still damp, but calmer. The ground is cold and hard.

"They add dirt on everything, stain us with lies, and you know what? At times, I believe the lies they say. Don't ever let it crawl in your ears. I'm lower than dirt, only smart as a horse, we are nothing. But when you think about it, we rooks are much, much more. Just look at you, child. You smart. You like them, and they fear that. More importantly, rook is like a symbol that been passed around for a long time through songs and poetry. A powerful message to us to keep our heads up for a better day. Some acquire rook as a name or maybe replace they slave names. We all know it gives great honor to know the roots of the rooks that is our ancestors. Not sure how it came alive, let's say me. I'm smart like that, but a poem was created. Do you know it?"

"We no crook but they shook. Dark as a raven books cast aside the rooks. We live but only through the nook. Pray our babies don't shook. Lawd, we see what's to come. We read your black book, the ones with the signs heavenly. Righteousness, freedom, thou shalt love one another till the stars themselves crumble. Stay strong, my dear rooks. The ravens see our look. Stay humble, my dear rook. Cast your hooks for a new tomorrow. Despair may come but a brighter day still follows."

Bo chimes in, "Lawd, o lawd, forgive us rooks."

# Chapter 19

Early in the morning, we are back at it. Some plant as others pick the cotton. The young girls are churning milk, making butter outside of the biggest cabin. The two overseers, Jonathan and Redd, circle around watching us like eagles. The sun is merciless and relentless.

"Water!" I yell.

"Hi, I'm Cliff. Here." He drops the bucket.

My eyes grow big. "You're Cliff? I know your Mama."

He looks at me with disgust. "Hand me another spoonful. Thanks."

I try to talk to him. "She's wonderful. Please understand where she came from."

He keeps shaking his head no.

"Look, not long ago, I lost someone close to me. I didn't get a chance to fix our problem, but you have all the time in the world."

"What happen? Why you not fix it?" He has a soft voice, but a slash going from his left ear to his cheek. He is no taller than my hip and might be one of the smallest boys.

"She died, and we were so close. All she wanted was to apologize but I never gave her a chance."

Redd comes over. "Stop talking, you pathetic rooks." Redd's posture demands obedience. His nose flares.

"I gots to go." His small figure turns from Redd.

"No! Wait," I holler. My back aches, reaching for him.

"But he get mad and beat us if me you talk."

I become stupid and careless, but I have to say what is on my mind, "That's fine. You listen, and I'll talk. Don't say a word, okay?"

He nods, up then down.

"Shut your mouth, darkies, last warning."

I'm not sure who yelled those commands.

"All I'm saying is don't be mad at your mama. She did her best. Let her back in, okay?"

Redd gets off the horse. "That's it. You can't stay out of trouble. I have something special for you!" He spits out a twig from his mouth. "Come here."

"Stay here," Redd says. He walks past the sad tree towards the kitchen cabin. The cabin has steps, unlike the small shacks, and two windows on each side of the door.

Redd returns with two buckets. "Hold these exactly how I am." Both of his arm make the letter T, with one pail in each. "Drop it any lower than that and you will regret it." He towers over me.

I stand still for a long time. Everyone is still working. I'm trembling intensely. My arms feel heavy and awkward. My strength fades and instantly he slashes at me.

"Ow." My brown dress dances in the air.

I hold on for far too long, gritting my teeth. My breathing is like a hissing noise. I swish my tongue around, hoping to produce saliva. I suppose he saw my struggle of thirst.

"You thirsty?" His tone is unconcerned. Redd's blue eyes shimmer with deceit. He goes for another pail. "Stay still."

I drop my arms the moment he turns around. When I hear the door shut, my arms spring to life.

Redd is carrying another bucket. It looks lighter by the way he is walking. "Thirsty, right?"

I nod.

He folds his sleeves back up then unbuckles his belt, pissing in the wooden pail. The stench stings my nose.

"Drink if you get thirsty." He attaches it to my neck. I stand still as he rains down his act of cruelty. "Niggers will learn to respect their Kings! Do as you are told." He clicks his tongue. "I will break you until you can't stand." He cracks his whip at my feet. "Don't move!"

The stench of the bucket is strong as I crinkle my nose, holding my breath. My stomach is uneasy. I begin to wobble at the knees and shortly topple over. I can't comprehend what is worse, him abusing me or the humiliation. His laughter does not help much.

"Redd, let the girl go," Dante says.

"Why are you so soft, Dante? Have a backbone." He grunts past him. "Remember you are just our property."

I bathe, eat, then sleep.

The next day I decide to ask the mistress to look after Ina. Mary Ann lets me in. "What's your name, girl?"

"Abel, Ma'am." I slowly bow and go my way. "By the way, that was beautiful."

Her long yellow hair flings around. April is in a pretty green dress, the type with puffy shoulders. Her white gloves are on the stool. She is a tall slim woman.

"What, don't tell me you have an interest in the piano?"

I nod.

"You have a keen ear, child. How about this?" She continues, playing another.

I quietly applaud when she finishes.

"What piece fancies your taste, Abel?"

"Beethoven, miss."

She starts to play, "This one?"

"No, not that."

April plays a different tune and then again looks my way.

I rapidly shake my head. "May I, mistress?"

Her face leaps with astonishment. Her jaw drops. "You play?"

I walk to the keys and play exactly what comes to memory. It isn't much, but I assume she has a pretty good picture.

"Beethoven's Fur Elise. Wow, that was impressive. Even I couldn't do that until recently. Bagatelle in A Minor. One of his best pieces, a true master in his arts."

"Thank you again, mistress." I leave.

Sundays, Massa has us rest. I walk around, seeing what everyone doing. On this plantation, washing is done differently. Everyone boils their clothing in huge iron pots. They beat it to remove soap then repeat with boiling. The air smells nice and spicy. I wonder if it's coming from the smokehouse or the kitchen. The smokehouse is the only brick building beside the Meade's home. The smokehouse has a chimney.

I see soap being made in a huge container. "How do you make soap?" I ask.

"Benjamin is my name." His hand is firm.

"Abel."

He is an old man. His cheeks sag. He is in jeans and suspenders with a straw hat.

"Ain't no one care bout your name. She ask how is it done."
The old lady hits Benjamin.

"Hi dear. I'm Patsy. We know you. Remember Ludo night?
Anyway, child you need lye and fat 'n good stirring. Smell that?"
Her surprisingly small nostrils flare.

It smells like flowers. I almost want to lick the pink liquid.

Patsy's voice is bumpy and bossy. She uses her blue apron to
wipe the sweat from her forehead. Her gray hair is long for her
old age. Her eyes are surrounded with wrinkles.

"Abel! Abel!" Aunty is charging my way, holding her dress,
as if I have her seal for freedom and a ticket out. "You won't
believe this. My boy, Cliff, he came to me and . . ." she breaks
out in a song. "I don't know what happen, but we spoke like
how we use to, not how it be now. Hallelujah. Lawd good."

I'm ecstatic for her. That's how it should be.

Late in the evening, we start a fire to relax. Everyone but the
inside women joins. The fire struggles to burn as it is dimly lit.
Lonny did a poor job at it. I start to study my hands.

"Apple, what troubles you?" My ears twitch, ignoring what
I wanted to say. "Nothing, just missing some few people. Wondering if we will ever get out of this."

"Eat up, guys!" We have cooked meat on a stick and fried
pepper on a stick, potatoes on a stick, you name it. The new
wood starts to crack, giving new life to the roaring fire. "That's
how you start a fire." The lot of them shout but are only teasing her.

My new family helps me adjust to my life of a chained rook. They say the key to surviving is to never give up. But I've already given up, haven't I?

All gather around the fire. The elderly tell stories. The few people with a banjo outside their shacks start to play.

Someone else starts playing the flute, dancing. "You guys know this one." She starts to sing. Everyone joins in. Aunty, Bo, and Cliff are singing. The young boy has a sweet voice. I keep quiet, not knowing the words.

Aunty and I sit under the giant tree. It's not so sad in the evening. "Uncle, where you from?" Only way I can tease her.

"Uncle, huh? Okay, fair. Ghana. I remember walking about in the woods, then ended up here. Never saw my folks. They don't know if I dead or none. You, child?"

"Missouri." My muscles tighten. Stolen from my parents as well. "Aunty, I hate to ask but that cut on your chin—"

"I needed to see if I was alive. After losing my babies. Actually, more like if I wanted to live. I couldn't feel much . . . I—" She pauses, and I lean up closer back against the tree. All I see are her eyes and teeth.

"Will it ever end?"

"I'm sorry, Abel. I honestly don't think so. I be forty and still have the taste of chains in the back of my throat. No, it does not end."

"You're so old." Her grin brightens the night.

# Chapter 20

After work is done, I run to Bo. "Bo, do you think all of us can play Ludo? Me, you, Cliff, and Aunty."

"Of course. Go tell Aunty and Cliff. I will set it up. Meet in our lovely shack." Bo's head still shines bald. The lash on his arm is thick and awful.

However, that is how my back feels. Every time I run my hands down it, I tear up. I have the same back as Mama has, except hers has no end.

Massa has a meeting with a few colleagues. Several stage-coaches pull up. Four men step out, two in each. The youngest, though tallest, on the far right has a gold pocket watch in his hands. The man next to him has a limp to his stride. His suit is black with a red bowtie. The cigar in his hands has smoke escaping from the ashes.

"Gentlemen!" Dante and Monta shout as they all go in the house.

"I want the red piece!" I claim quickly. "It's his favorite color."

"Blue for me," Aunty says next.

Bo picks up the green piece.

I'm first, then Cliff, Bo, and Aunty. "You need to roll a six to get out, right?" My first roll is a five. I can't move any token pieces.

"Oh, close," the little one says.

Bo is the only one to roll a six, so he is out first.

"Abel, it was a fine idea to give Ina to mistress until you ready. Even though I already said so," Aunty mocks.

"I just wanted her to stay in a cozy place. Besides, the mistress was nice to me when I saw her. She even let me play her piano."

Their heads jerk up. "You?"

"I had a friend who was very brilliant at it. I learned a song but nothing too impressive."

Bo rolls the dice on the glass.

Cliff huddles in a blanket. His scrawny neck is all I see.

I did not notice before, but their shack smells nice. They have an open jar of that pink soap set in the far corner.

Bo is the only one with a piece out. He easily goes around the board.

"How is this possible nobody can get a six?"

Bo laughs with his tongue out. "That's what ya'll get."

"I have a six, Papa," Cliff says. The dice clearly mark five, but we let him on the board anyways. Aunty and him high five each other.

It's Bo's turn. He makes it home. Three green token pieces are left for him.

Aunty gets on, then I finally do.

Aunty asks, "How did you become like the white men with your fancy talk?"

I wait for him to go. "I had a teacher. She taught me. We were always on and off because her lessons were always complicated. She was splendid. She always read to me. I also had a friend and we were aggressive when it came to education. I miss him, too. He is the same friend that plays the piano."

"Sorry, child. She seems wonderful. They both do. Think you can teach my boy some smarts? I want him to grow up like you. You know something, yous can prove to Massa that your worth something. Show him off, somehow. I like to see that! We more than they think."

"Only if you let me win. Blow on the dice, please. Is Massa a good man?" I ask. I'm lying on my stomach. Aunty and Bo are sitting on their butts and Cliff is still cozy with his blanket.

"Well, he better than my first owner."

"I'm still not letting you win with your sweet talk, Bo."

I ask them a question. "How did y'all make this game?"

Aunty answers, "We had Mary Ann help us steal paper and other supplies. She head servant for Massa. She like my older sister. We always adore each other, learn a lot from her but always bicker at each other too. It's been hard to see one another. As you can see, the game easy to create."

"We gots ourselves a game now," Bo howls with excitement.

I roll another six and decide to have two pieces out just in case one is eaten. I still will be free if I can't roll another six. Whenever there are two pieces out, you can switch between either one. Cliff is two spaces ahead of me. I wait for my turn hoping the dice will roll a two. No luck, a three comes. I move my piece. What are the odds of him landing a one?

"Son, eat her! Eat her." Phew, he just missed me when his turn came around. Bo gets a piece safely around the board and to home base. Aunty keeps rolling ones and she is moving nowhere.

I eventually eat Cliff after our exciting near-misses and he becomes my worker.

Bo starts going crazy with his big self. "One more piece, guys. Come on. Y'all make this super easy. Guess I will win once more." His tongue sticks out.

A woman stands at the door.

"What it be, Mary Ann?" Aunty and Bo ask.

I look back. She is a tall older woman. She has dark brown hair and soft pink lips. A teardrop earring hangs from her ears, one of the few I noticed who have their ears pierced. She's wearing her housemaid outfit.

"Massa real mad. I be serving supper and his friends kept pestering him about being a weak. They say, you have to control us not let us be wild. He so angry! They also ask what he done about you three when the escape happened. Guys, I don't know what Massa might do."

Bo looks at Mary Ann. "We suffered for that already. Remember? That happen three moons ago. Why now?"

"I know, I know. But his people, his pride. I think they got to him. His mind easily sways. They want more than just lashes."

"No, not my boys, not my family! I'll take whatever he dishes, least I can do."

"Antebellum, Bo, come out here now!" Massa screams loud enough to hear him.

"Stay here, Cliff." I hold the young child. They leave us behind.

"The boy as well. Don't test my patience." His voice appear to be a lot closer now.

When I step out, there are five males holding guns with expressions wanting blood.

"Is it ready yet?" Dante yells.

"Yes, Father, it's ready."

It is darker than I thought. There are a couple of pine torches lit in front of the shacks.

"Look Massa, we done get punish already. Have a heart," Bo pleads. They bring three pieces of lumber, each going up and another tied across from it.

"Get them. Tie 'em up."

Bo swings at them when they lay their hands on his son and wife but is shortly beaten into submission.

"Gather around. Gather around! This is exactly what happens when you try to run or disobey me. I will not tolerate the insubordination of you filths."

They had dug three small holes right in front of his big home. The tree in front of his house has never looked sadder. The wood made the letter 'T.' All three of them were tied down and raised.

Massa continues. "They will hang here till morning. None best untie or feed them."

His sinful son croaks, "Father is that the best you can do? Just look. They are not impressed at all."

The men's faces are dull.

His son whispers something to him. I can tell Dante is disgusted but he orders him to go get something.

Aunty says, "Please Massa, let my boy free. He only be a child."

It almost appears as if he will, but then one of his friends says, "Dante, don't be weak. Show them who's in charge or lose your status! How will your slaves ever respect a man that's a coward?"

"Gentlemen, have patience."

Monta comes back, a whiff of nastiness following him.

"Go ahead, son." Without any hesitation everyone begin to beg.

"Massa, please! They learn they lesson! Don't do this! We work for free if it's about money. We eat less. What it be, Massa?"

All three are dangling. The smell of burning wood floods my nostrils. The burning heat surges my way.

His colleagues watch in amazement. "Yes, my boy! Simply marvelous," they exclaim.

Helpless, they lose hope, screaming in the most gruesome way. They still beg to let the boy go.

April comes out holding her long dark blue dress. "What are you doing?"

Her husband does not bother to respond to her.

"Dante!" She runs to him, only to eat grass.

Dante's hands return to his pockets. "Mother, not now. It's best if you go back inside."

She seems to like us, but has the luxury to look elsewhere.

The fire builds, eating the wood and approaching their boots.

One thought comes to mind.

I stand in front of everyone with a voice that reaches the heavens. "We no crooks but they shook!" I shout at the top of my lungs! "Dark as a raven books cast aside the rooks."

Aunty, Bo, and their son focus on me and speak with agonizing torment in their voice. The scent is strong enough to make you walk away.

Massa stands with a stale expression, wearing all red. The gums of Monta's teeth shine with delight.

"We fly high but only through the nook. Lord, we see what's to come we read your black book! Righteousness, freedom, thou shalt love one another till the stars themselves crumble!"

Three voices disappear.

"Stay strong, my dear rooks. The ravens see our look. Stay humble, my dear rook. Cast your hooks for a new tomorrow."

Mary Ann falls down to her knees, pounding on the ground, pulling grass, pulling her hair, her mouth kissing the dirt. "They gone, they gone! Why? Lawd, why?"

I stick my hands out. "Despair may come but a brighter day still follows."

Mary Ann grabs hold. "Lawd, O lawd forgive us rooks."

Aunty looks at me, with her final words, "Thank you. Live on Abel!"

They took the Father, the Son, and the Spirit, the Mother, along with my faith.

# Chapter 21

I cannot see colors anymore. Everything is black and white. I lose it all and become like Corjo. At every meal, the food is tasteless. The cooks are wonderful, but I cannot seem to enjoy much.

We slave day in and out. My mind is focused on work, so I don't have to taste the poisonous whip—so I don't have to think. The irrational thought of picking cotton is stronger than before. Even though I make weight, I still have this sense—a feeling that a noose is around my neck. My heart thumps and my throat dries as my mouth is relinquished of moisture. When I'm up to weigh my sack, the noose tightens.

It's not just me. We rooks look so depressed but it's understandable—our family has turned to ashes right before our eyes. Every time I inhale, I still smell their burning flesh. The white men act like nothing ever happened, more of a nuisance out the way.

In my shed, lying on my side, I close my eyes and try to escape. Antebellum was more than just a slave, she held the spirit of most, including me. She picked up my broken pieces and now she is a dust of my memory, but she won't blow away; none of them will. Bo was the father to us, the biggest one but still the gentlest. If you believe I was the first they spared cotton to, well then, you don't know them well.

What they call life feels more like drowning, living in constant sorrow but no one can pull us from the gray depths of the ocean. Cliff was like a son for most, the child who ran his fastest just to make sure we had water. He made sure we had the strength to continue. He had a smile that promised a new day would come when all men are equal. No, all men and women are equal. I feel at fault for telling him he has all the time in the world.

I feel the tears trying to force their way out through my closed eyelids. The heavy taps of rain hit the shack. Then comes the annoyance of it dripping through a small crack, making the dirt soft.

The sun lost its color. I lost the three that came to my aide on many occasions, the people that shared their life with me. May they rest in peace. They had been fighting for so long. Let them take flight with the ravens and soar the skies and protect the rest.

I've yet to see my family. I'm not sure but it might be plenty more years to come. I cannot seem to find the strength to continue. It hurts too much. Massa sold many people. Many new faces arrive, but it's easier to keep my distance. Why trouble myself with a life that can change any second by a man that has ownership over us. I might as well have a gun at my head at all times. Whenever it seems like I get close to someone, they just up and disappear, never to be seen again. Where do they go? Georgia, Mississippi, or maybe Florida?

Abel, get a hold of yourself. It hurts.

Ina and I are lucky to still have each other. It's been lonesome but every now and then I think about my parents, hoping they are still around and are free in the same house, never to be bothered again. All I want at this point is for Ina to meet them, rejoice, talk to them. I want to have a Thanksgiving dinner, one that includes a big meal with everyone.

I'd like to pour my soul out to my loved ones, if I may.

Aunty, you were like my second mother but seeing how strong you are, I realize my flaws lie deep in the roots. If I should perish by the white men, I want you to know that you plunged yourself into the ocean and fought those dangerous creatures and pulled me out along with Ina. I was at the point of letting her drown with me, but your wings carried us out. Because of you, and only you, I was beginning to see colors.

I see no happy ending for me, but I will live. I will live for her and you. They think slavery will break us, but they are wrong. Like the other rooks, I will be the raven that shines a light on my people. Maybe not today, maybe not tomorrow, but someday! If I should somehow get out of this, your story will be told.

Oh, Aunty, why? Aunty, if you allow me, I would like to hide you in this secret location. It's a door with an opening underneath the floor and we could talk until tomorrow stops existing until we are tired of each other. I only hope we have that luxury.

I'm past the point of pain. Everything feels numb. It's hard to breathe. What's beyond grief? Getting called a pathetic nigger doesn't bother me, but you know what? Getting called a pathetic rook, that's what gets me. I will not allow another to disrespect what you taught me. It's funny, I feel like I'm over thirty. Like I've aged drastically. I remember how I used to see them white children with toys and I stood outside the window. I also remember how I wanted to know how my own Ma felt, but I think I know. From what I can see, living every day must have been a grim struggle.

Pa, you are the one I sought for help—my mountain. I never wanted Ma to see me cry but to you, I pour my heart out. Papa, give your mind a rest; no one blames you. I promise to tell Ina about you. I talked my whole life with you, so I know your story. But Pa, I want you to tell me that everything is going to be all right because I don't know anymore. It seems like I walked into a cave and it collapsed behind me. It's so cold. I'm so scared, Pa. Demons lurk everywhere. Let me know you're okay, taking care of Mama. Pa, if I were blindfolded and you led me, you would avoid a twig in my path, just so no harm came my way. I chose to go another way, despite your teaching, and for that I'm sorry, but it's not my fault. I'll be the grown-up my sister needs. No more crying. I'll stay strong and independent.

Dear Ma, stay strong. I have faith I will see you once again. I'll take you to New York like I promised. You see, when I was looking at that window in the toy store, it wasn't the toys I wanted, no. What I wanted was this noose off my mother's neck. There are plenty of times to play with toys. I want the keys to her chains! I want to be the shoulder she cries on! I want life to be given back to her, give her the youth she deserves, let her be the kid that looks through that window, wishing for that doll. How many times did you scream no? How many others laid their bodies on yours? How are you so strong? Mama, when I said I'll take care of Ina, this is not what I meant. This is not what I want. I'm not upset but if I had a wish, Ma, I want the voice I never got a chance to hear.

# Chapter 22

Ladder year of 1861

I've been summoned. Mistress wants to see me. I walk up to their porch. The weird statue of the headless kid has leaves on it.

I see Dante The Inferno playing chess with his friend. I slowly walk up his steps.

"I wouldn't move your bishop there. That's precisely what he wants, sir."

He shrugs me off. "Quiet, girl. You know nothing of this intellectual game." Dante stubs his cigar out on the table. His friend is a slim old man with snow-white hair. He leans over to make his move.

"Yes, Massa. Sorry for the troubles."

His brow lowers as I breeze past.

A new house servant is guiding me. I do not bother to get her name. She guides me up the right steps then straight ahead to a white door and opens it for me.

I see Ina walking around, looking happy. "Abel, glad you're here. I want you to work inside. This way you can be with your daughter and help me. How does that sound?"

Dante walks in. "Absolutely not. This girl has been hiding the fact that she is educated to some degree."

"So what, dear? She can help Ariana learn."

I nod, agreeing with the mistress.

"So, you knew all along? I will not have this pathetic roo-"

I cut him off before he could taint the word any further. "Massa, if I am so pitiful, allow me to show you in the intellectual game of chess, that only you can play." I was daring but chose my words carefully. "If I should lose, sell me! But if I should win, I never want that word to even touch your lips. You will address us differently. Call us filth, call us maggots but don't you dare call us rooks!"

My posture is firm. He can strike me down, but I won't wince.

"Be careful, you little wench."

He may be Dante the Inferno, but my fire sears hotter than the sun. He is only a campfire that just got started. If I should piss on him, he will smolder out.

"Very well, Abel. If you should lose, I will sell you and your daughter to different families. Deal?"

"How do I know you are a man of your word?"

He walks closer to me and extends his hand. "A gentleman never goes back on his handshake. Plus, this will be a promise to my lord and savior."

I shake his lukewarm hand. Now I could have asked for our freedom, but that's another fantasy that won't come true.

This is for you, Aunty. I'll show him.

The board is brought in. "Thank you, Josephine. You may go now," Dante says.

"Sir, if I may, can I stay?"

He tells her, "Very well." Our witnesses are April and her child along with mine and the servant Josephine. "You can have the black pieces," he tells me.

"I always use the white pieces if I may, Massa."

"Stubborn child. Very well, come then. Flip for the first move." He pulls a silver coin out of his pocket. I tell him to go first. "Cocky." He tells me while searching for a move.

It is not about being cocky. For me, it's having the patience to analyze every possible outcome. I'm not nervous in the least but there is a lot on the table.

I point to four pieces—the king, my queen, and two rooks. "You will not take these."

My opponent is tough but lacks grace. He is the cocky one and that will be his downfall. He is a simple man and does not cherish his pieces. He brings out his pawns as if they were mere servants to do his bidding. As for me, I take my time and only sacrifice what is needed. I look at Ina whenever I sweep a piece with my rook. I think about Papa when I retreat my king, and Ma, the fiercest of them all.

"Massa, what's the difference between a raven and an eagle?" I say in a low, dull tone. Happiness slithers out of me.

"What are you babbling on about? There are no differences. They are both birds, equal species."

Piece by piece we kill.

He grunts something when he retreats his knight. He watches for my next move. His red eyes flicker.

"I just thought I'd ask. I cannot seem to wrap my head around the idea either."

The board jumps with joy when we swiftly toss our army around. Tacticians at war. I don't have to think about my next move. It's like my eyes are shut and I play with my mind. I have him in check and the rook does the final blow. My eyes are dangerous. I allow myself to absorb power.

The vision of the game is my two rooks surrounding his king. My king in the far distance, ready to retaliate. The only part that did not come true is my queen; he managed to swipe her. Was I careless? I tried to get a pawn across and get my queen back, but I had no time. His rook put up a fight but couldn't hold its own.

"She won, Dante."

He looks at his wife. She is in awe.

"She is marvelous. I'm quite speechless. A toast." He pulls out a glass and pours himself some scotch. He offers me the golden liquid.

I don't want to take a sip, but then again, I do not want to be rude.

He makes a toast. "To new beginnings."

My face turns sour and my throat is burning. It's awful.

"After today, you will work with my wife in the house, take care of your child, but on the weekends, you will return to the fields. I will be in my study if anyone needs me." He passionately kisses his wife then kisses his child on the forehead and goes his way.

Ina has grown so much through the years. She's walking and just barely talking. I keep an eye on her, but the mistress spends the most time with her.

"Abel, this is Ariana. She is two years old. Your daughter has become real close friends with my baby."

Like I said, there is no difference. The babies aren't corrupted, so why is one in a cage? I walk up to my sister and deliver a hug. It feels like home.

Mistress plays on her black piano that looks as if it is slathered in fresh black paint. "Abel, I will soon venture to the market. I'd like you to accompany me."

"Yes, mistress."

She walks out the room. "Stay here."

When April Meade comes back, she has a new outfit for me, one that is not like the house servants, but it makes me feel alive. It is a long black dress with a blue corset that chokes me, white gloves, and a plaid scarf. For the first time, I'm wearing shoes with full laces and buttons. They fit nicely too.

April is alluring too. She is wearing the opposite of me, a long blue dress and black corset. She has her emerald necklace around her neck. She is all soft lines and subtle curves; it's elegant. Her hair is tied in a gold band.

The driver is waiting. He is a white man with a dark black coat on, dark boots, and a long hat. We leave in a carriage.

"We need supplies for the dinner party tonight, more wine and meat." She sweeps her dress under, making room for me. I sweep my dress from under and scoot in.

The carriage is rocky. "Abel, do not be afraid to speak openly with me. I want to talk about your friends. My truest of apologies. Even I have no authority. However, I have no right to compare myself to you. Would you believe me if I said that if I could have stopped them, I would?"

I look at her. "Yes, I do. The way you play your music speaks for you. I think only beautiful hearts that care for another can play beautiful songs."

"Thank you. You are stunning, you know that?"

I blush. "I like your hair tied like that."

April laughs a bit.

"Almost there, Madam Meade."

# Chapter 23

"Looks like we are here. After this, you can help polish my nails." The rocking stops and I look outside. There are so many people around. This is my first time outside of the Meade plantation. The city is lively and reminds me of Welton town. "Come now, Abel. Don't get left behind."

The air smells fresh and clean. The crowds are loud. Merchants holler at people walking by. The mistress is well liked.

"Good afternoon, Mrs. Meade. How are you today?" Hats are tipped, women smile or kiss her on both cheeks. It's amazing what having a bit of money can do. They are all well-groomed.

April buys her supplies and I hold the bags. I see a thief running.

"Stop that man, someone help me!" The white-haired man's voice is lost in the crowd. The man running is in a thick dark coat. It was another white man stealing from his own. Not in a bad way, but it's funny.

"What's so funny?" April asks.

"I'm enjoying the little things, taking in the fresh air." The market is vast. I see an array of pig heads nailed to a wooden stand. Fish cut in three different sections is set on another stand. There is a barrel of pineapples. The sky is filled with gawking birds.

I hear loud noises come from a distance. With concern, I ask, "What's all the noise coming from over there?" I point.

Her cheeks flush red. "It's probably an auction. Let's go back. We are done here."

I beg her to stay, not sure why but I needed to see from the outside. Just as I thought, it is the same sight. There is nothing beautiful about slavery. I've heard the stories, I have witnessed it, and now I am observing through the nook of my mistress. Each are three different scenarios, but the same feeling always surfaces, dreadful.

I believe we are behind a church. The building is huge and pointy at the top. I have a grimy taste in my mouth like the slop they fed me at my auction. It is enough to keep me moving, keep my stomach from arguing with me. I hear crying and some laughter all mixed together. It is a gloomy event that should never be portrayed. If a slave family happens to stay together, how long will it be? A year, maybe a month. Then that fragment of happiness is torn right from their clutches. Slaves are constantly whipped or starved. I don't think that should ever be a conversation nor a time when I have to convince my sister to stay strong. What does one even say to bring hope back, everything will be fine? At least its only ten lashes? We tell themselves lies to move on. April and I stand in the back. I drop the bags as I watch.

The rooks' shadows tell another story when the sun flashes. It's like their shadows convey concealed emotions—the past, maybe future, feelings each of them embody.

I can tell a single man or woman's shadow is scared but knows that they have nothing to lose. The slaves that are by themselves, they already lost a family. Their shadows are as vacant as the face they carry. The young one's shadow emerges with hope yet baffled. It dances and trembles in a bizarre way to cope with whatever is sizzling in their minds.

Mothers' or fathers' shadows always cast the same way, no matter the amount of sunlight that strikes at their feet. Each shadow of a parent is like polka dots. There is one dot at their aching heart, wondering was it even worth having children? Two more dots at their eyes, watching, living, and breathing the fact that they are the last kin since their babies are long gone. A light pierces through mothers' and fathers' heads because hope is lost—a shattered dream that manifests into nightmares. The idea that their own children are now memories, never to be held again. Will the kids remember who birthed them? They have become just a name, and what's a name without a face?

I wonder what my shadow says. Did it shake, knowing my dreams would turn to sand or do I have an ounce of happiness knowing my sister is still with me? Were there fractures that penetrated deeply as I stood on the stage by myself, holding Ina? What about Ina? She won't remember Ma and Pa.

"Abel, are you okay?" Mistress breaks me out my thoughts.

My hand is trying to hold back the vomit that desires to come out.

I see a helpless mother fighting over her family. Every desperate punch she throws is a story in itself, sorrow, anger—she knows nothing will help. It takes several people to settle the argument. However, only one side voices their opinion. "Mamaaa!"

"Yes, I'm okay. May I say something? I hope you don't take it the wrong way."

She waves me a go ahead.

"What do you think about all this?"

"My grandma always told me we are like salt. I comprehended what she meant when I grew up. Do you know the meaning of unpalatable? Basically, not a pleasant taste. The thing about salt is if you apply too much it becomes an ugly meal, right? People . . . I mean, Americans, don't know how to make our meal flavorful. We don't know when and how to stop adding and tainting everything that we own, but that's not the right word. We should not own another. I cook and prepare many meals, and salt is not the only ingredient present. Sorry, I never get a chance to voice my opinion, but it's a disgusting notion."

"It's fine, can we stay a bit longer?" I'm not feeling well. Slaves are dancing for the crowd, showing their worth, trying to preserve the only thing we know, family.

"Dinner is served," Mary Ann shouts.

"Splendid. Marvelous," Dante says. The guests and family leisurely come in and take their seats. We have everything set up. I've been learning from Mary Ann how to properly set the table and prepare meals. Napkins on one side, glass on the other. I know the proper placement for silverware. The boys position themselves in those boxes right above the table.

"More wine, please," Dante's friend orders.

Josephine is in charge of passing out the beverages from the rack filled with many different bottles.

I, on the other hand, wait for a simple task if they should command it. I am going back and forth, switching out dishes. "Mary Ann, they are all wondering how long the steak will take. What should I tell them?"

"Five more minutes, dear. They like it cooked properly, none of that red juice all over."

I bust out and race to the opposite side of the hall to the table and tell them. There are ten at the table, including the three members of the Meade family.

Angelica, April's friend, is there also, sitting beside April. She, too, has blonde hair. Her facial structure is sturdy, and she is wearing a brown dress matching her eyes.

"Gentlemen. Ladies. This is the girl that has the right mind-set for chess." They look at me like an exhibit.

"A nigger playing chess—preposterous. That's like a monkey sipping and pouring tea on a leisurely Sunday afternoon," the old man with the pig nose said, chuckling and smacking the table.

It is a calm evening. They sit at the table discussing work, but each has their own motives, wanting to outshine the next. I see it through their beards and mustaches. The breeze from the boys' fans is delicate.

Monta won't stop glaring at me. His gaze sends shivers down my neck and then some. The food is well-presented and smells wonderful. I wish I could eat too. They have hot buns, fish doused in herbs and seasoning, and fried onions. The steak is still steaming. Hot cheese is melted on top with fried peppers on the side.

"Abel, my cup is empty." Monta puts out his glass. He slams it on the table, shaking the spoons and plates.

I firmly place another hand over the bottle, trying to ease my shaking hands but I can't stop myself. He waves his pointer finger around. "Ah, ah, ah, careful now. Don't want to tarnish my new suit." Monta grins at me.

I take a deep breath and pour. "Is this enough, Massa? How about now, Massa?" A droplet hits the table.

"It's okay, dear. You may go. It's only a small spill. Nothing to fuss." I look at April but then she starts a conversation with one of her lady friends.

They wipe the grease off their hands and mouth. A few belch with satisfaction.

"Joe, may I see you in my study?" Joe Turner, married to Angelica, is an average looking man in a gray wool suit and trousers.

"What for? I was just about to leave. This better be a pressing matter, Dante. Wait for me, dear." The gentleman tosses his rag on the table after wiping his mouth and digging through his fingernails. The others leave.

"The war that's about to be issued. I want to hear your thoughts. I think I might support the south with a supply of money. I'm quite baffled about this turn of events."

"Come, April," Angelica says.

The house servants clean up after them and the boys with the fans hop down.

"Clean and wipe the tables. Make sure it's spotless and someone dust around here." Mary Ann glides her hand on a shelf and points at her dirty finger.

"You sure that's not your skin, Ann?" Josephine says. We laugh at the poor joke. She is a scrawny girl with lips as black as her hair.

Mary Ann looks my way. "I miss them so much."

I walk towards Ann. "How about a game of Ludo? It's been a while since we played."

She nods in agreement. We finish cleaning and go to Josephine's quarters to play. Another servant, Mildred, plays with us. She is around my age, maybe a tad older. Josephine's room is not much. She has a mattress with four pillars and white fabrics on top plus a closet and two cabinets.

Josephine pitches in her thoughts. "Know what? I hate the feeling when you sleep real good but you know you gotta pee! But I just don't bother myself, not saying I wet myself, none that. However, I rather sleep. Why wake up to this, it actually pains me to get up."

Amen.

Mildred is a quiet mouse. "Is . . . is it my turn?"

I'm not sure, but I think she feels uncomfortable around us because she looks more white than black. Her dark hair is short. She has white wraps covering her whole arm, reaching to the sleeves of her purple sleeves. Her neck is scorched like Malcolm's.

Mildred does not know any of her family. She told us that her father ran away. But it was a white lady that took care of her. She always took her out of any danger and made sure she had plenty to eat.

Josephine asks, "So Ann, you and Amaka seem to be getting along quite nicely."

Ann looks around the room. "Keep your voice down. The last thing I need is they blowing hot air about. Besides, you best roll me a five now!"

Josephine rolls a one and sticks out her tongue.

"Josephine?"

"Yes, Massa!" She tells us to hide in her closet. "Don't make a sound and no matter what, don't come out. It's late, Massa. I'm tired. Please let me sleep. Not today."

"Drop the dress, Josephine. Don't make me say it again!"

Josephine is halfway naked, arms across her breast, trembling with fear.

He sees me. His head jerks like the long hand on a clock. "What are you doing here?"

I take a gulp and move away from the closet door, trying to hide the rest. I respond quickly and crisply, exerting no fault. "I came to find a dress. The mistress wants me to look real fancy. She taking me out again." I keep my eyes down, showing no disrespect. His hands come from underneath her dress.

"No shoes, what you hear?" His breath is foul.

"Nothing, I swear. That door makes you go deaf. Look, you can even go in to check for yourself."

He backs away and Josephine conceals herself. There is a brand of some kind below her right shoulder. The door slams. Josephine drops to her bedside, shaking.

"How long he come in like that?" Ann asks, rage flowing through her tone. "That man will get what he deserves."

"Don't look at me like that, Mildred," Josephine roars.

"He gets what's comin," Ann says.

I don't think there is much I can say to stop her even though I feel the same. "You okay?" I ask.

"No, I'm not." She points to the brand mark I saw earlier. "This one from long ago, my first brand. They toss me down on a bed of rocks. The W.W. is from Wilson Walker." She points to another right around her ribs. "This here was for fun, I remember that day. I was sold to a new owner. I only mind my business changing in peace then he walks in on me. Drags me to a stable. I thought he be done and happy but wanted to show more, took a hot iron and press against my body. Said I was his conquest, branded his flag. And this last one when I decided to run. I paid it all. All from my Massa's till sold here."

On her back was something that resembled Mother's. "I cannot take no more. They just use me as they so please." She went on all fours and hurled her grief. "I can't no more."

"Hush now child, we will," Mary Ann says.

# Chapter 24

I believe it's Friday or maybe Saturday, but I am at work plucking more cotton. I am getting reacquainted with Redd and Jonathan. A lovely pair those two are.

"How the house life be treating you, Abel?" Malcolm asks. He is a short guy, one of Bo's best buds. Malcolm has burn scars on the far side of his face that perpetually alters his features. He is one of the first slaves of the Meade plantation. Dante loves his crafting skills; they have made him plenty of money. I see Malcolm building wheels more than picking cotton.

The wind blows in strong, tossing my sack to the back of my hip. "It's a lot better than slaving out here. Nice and cool, too!"

That makes him chuckle. "Yeah, I bet. Happy for you. I been building and fixing broken wheels, anything I can do for some coins. Soon, I'll buy my freedom." He has a bright smile.

"Glad to hear. Praying for your freedom. How are the new guys?"

He points at someone dark as night. "He be having a rough time. Everyone does at first with this new life. I suppose reality kicks in later for the younger folks. He don't realize that we slaves to the white men and overseer. Don't worry, I helps him best I can."

"Bo and Aunty would be happy to hear that."

"Abel you . . . you think maybe I can learn? Get me some smarts. Thinking I might go north, join the war, fight for ya'll when I buy my freedom. I'd love to write back to everyone."

I hear the horses galloping. "Get back to work!" the overseer, Jonathan, says. He is chunky, wearing a plaid green shirt and gray trousers with brown boots.

I scream for water and we both take a sip. "I'm surprised you haven't asked earlier."

They holler at us to line up. The older folks are weary. I'm not sure how much they can take.

Later that day.

In my quarters, one of the maids comes in, pounding on my door. "Monta wants to see you."

I feel my stomach drop.

I walk up the steps. To the left is Monta's room. His door is shut. I knock softly.

"Come in." The creak of the door fills my ear.

"Ahh, Abel, won't you join me? I'd like to play you in a game." He has a chess board. "I set the game already and, of course, you are the black pieces." His board is real fancy with designs on the outer edges.

Monta's sanctuary has a big bed with black shiny posts. The walls are white and there is nothing more than a desk with spilled ink splotches that have dried up. The only beautiful art he has is the door that leads into the abyss. An abnormal odor comes from within, a smell that reeks like when your tub breaks. The smell floods my nose, almost making me tear up.

"I wish not to play you, if that's okay, Massa." I wait before I leave.

He slams his hand down on the small table. The pieces rustle.

I jump back.

"You are playing. Am I clear?" Monta fixes his dark blue tie.

I sit down and repeat once more, "I wish not to play."

He smacks me on my cheek. "You shit of a r . . ." He quakes in his dark shoes, looking dumbfounded. He stutters, "Don't s-s-s-stare at me like that. Besides, look behind you." He gives me a superior grin.

"Ina?" I rush over.

"Sit back down, Abel."

"You disgusting little man!"

"Watch your tongue. She is fine but after this, it's up to you to keep her safe." He pulls a gun on the table. Monta walks over to a record and sets it up. The most eerie sound fills the room.

"Shall we begin, since we know the stakes?"

This has become a really bad dream. Am I really playing for my sister's life?

His hands overlap across each other, one leg propped over the other. He leans his chair back.

Sweat drips from my forehead and underneath my armpits. My sister stares at me. I try to focus. A glimmer of fear rings through her body. I give her a fake mask, showing everything is okay.

"You may go first, Abel."

I shake, reaching for the first piece and hovering over my army. Knight, no, pawn. I'm not sure.

"Hurry up!" Monta demands.

I move the end pawn on my right one space.

"My father is very fond of you. Me, on the other hand, I could care less. Nothing but trash that I can throw out at any given time." He makes a move.

"Why are you doing this?" I ask.

He ignores me. His emerald eyes fix on the board.

I imagine myself in a dark wood that is filled with mist. I cannot hear a thing except the sound of horses chasing me or Ina's cry for help. Every time he moves a knight or his army, he chops at my throat. They are still chasing me. I dive deeper in the woods. The music is still menacingly strong.

Late in the game, I start to panic. The sour odor of my sweat beads along my cheeks.

"Are you playing me seriously? Remember now." He waves his gun aimlessly.

"Mama!"

I twist back, take a deep breath to calm my nerves. I need to get out of this dark forest. I hear Ina's voice in the far distance of the woods.

He moves a pawn. I take it with a bishop but that is a mistake. He outplays me. "Pawn for a bishop, how naive."

"So, it was your idea to burn my friends."

"What of it? Father lacks the strength to do anything right, so I stepped in. More food for you darkies, anyhow. You're welcome. My only regret is we should have taken off their shoes and clothes. How foolish of a waste. Am I wrong?" He laughs hysterically. Every word that he vomits out is like stepping in manure.

"They ran away three months ago. Their fault for running." His tone holds nothing, only icy roughness. Whenever he breathes, cold air seeps out and the forest becomes colder.

Okay, if I move this piece, his bishop can assassinate my move, but if I don't move this pawn, he can capture my knight. What if . . . no that won't work. What should I do? Think. Think!

This game is tough and not going well.

"Mama." Ina starts fussing around because her right arm is tied to his desk.

Monta gets a pawn across the murky swamp and revives a piece.

"Nervous, Abel? You're shaking like a leaf. Show me those skills Father mentioned." He moves a piece, yelling, "Check!"

My heart drums a beat and my foot is tapping uncontrollably. I can't hear Ina's voice. I am entangled by vicious vines.

"Nowhere to move."

I examine the board over and over. Is he right? No, keep looking! Ina, I'm coming. My heart is racing. I wipe my sweaty palms on my dress.

His gun is on the table. "I have one move left." I tell him. In the dark of the forest, I spot a lit torch and bolt at it.

"Where? I don't see a move," he cries out.

I reach for my rook, hover it above the board, then slide it across.

"If you do that, I'll take that piece."

Now or never. The fire is dying out!

I do as he thought and it's back to his turn. He reaches right. He has to extend on the other side for his finishing blow and I lunge for the gun.

We tussle for his weapon. I have the better grip. It is a whole new battle. We fight on the ground, both of our hands attached to the gun. He hits me, but I do not let go.

"Ina, baby, hang in there!" I keep shouting her name. The gun flops out of our hands. I crawl through the mist.

"Mama!" Ina screeches. The room is filled with screams of death. The record stops. I won't lose this time. I kick him where it hurts most.

He grabs me, halting my reach. I have lost. The fire dies out.

The door flies open. "Monta, what are you doing? I thought you wanted to play her in a friendly game? Put it down, son."

His family is here. I roll on the ground towards my sister.

"Father, stay out of this."

"Now, Monta, it's all right. I see now that Grandpa had a bad influence on you, but it's okay. Put the gun down."

I'm in front of Ina. April and her child are both at the scene as well as Mary Ann and Josephine. "Abel! Ina!"

I don't even look. I squeeze her small face, then Dante jumps in. It reminds me of Corjo and his father.

"Son, you need to take your medication. You're not healthy. Those stories Grandpa told you were all made up. Monta!"

"Drop the weapon!" April yells.

Monta begins to stutter, "See! S-sh-she never liked me. I told you to leave her." They are tossing back and forth, then all of sudden, the pistol fires like a loud cannon.

I said that I wouldn't cry. Unfortunately, I can't help it. My . . . she . . . "Get some towels now! Hang in there!"

# Chapter 25

Smoke rises from the pistol.

"Where are those towels?" Dante demands.

I spring alive like a predator in action. Down the hall, I open those big white twin door shelves filled with towels and supplies.

"Here, help her," I say.

"Mama, it hurts."

"I know, baby. Stay strong for me." A bullet is in her leg.

"Dante, I want that boy away from here. I don't ever want to see him. Mary Ann, get some help," April yells.

Weeks later, I sit down with April. "Are you going to be okay?"

"Yes, I'm glad that boy is gone. I tried to welcome him as my own, but he insisted on defying me."

I rub her back. Her smooth silk dress feels nice.

"He belonged to another woman. He was nothing but trouble ever since I met Dante. I suppose there was a time I called him my son. He never was right in the head. Dante hates to speak ill of his child, that proud man, but I did not want Monta to think I did not love him. He told me how his grandpa used to kill his servants, just crazy stuff like that." She sighs, remembering that day. "I am heading to the market. Abel, look after her for me. Oh, before I forget, there is a letter waiting for you. I left it on your dresser." She leaves her piano room.

Letter? I never did have a chance to read Margo Bell's letter. It sure would be nice to hear a familiar voice even if it's through paper.

I bring in a glass of water for Ariana and a sandwich made from wheat bread with a napkin on the side. Poor thing.

"Sit up, Ariana. Sip slower." She coughs out the water and wipes her face with her left hand. "Use this, hon. Doctor Williams is coming to see you."

Looking around, her bedroom is beautiful, unlike her brother's. Her sheets and pillows are pink silk. Everywhere I step, I almost twist an ankle due to her excessive belongings. A singular curtain waves because she never shuts the window.

"Abel, is Ina okay?"

I nod. Ariana wraps herself in her blanket.

"She's worried about you. Ina wants you to play with her like how you guys used to."

Underneath the blanket, she looks at her leg. "How can I? I cannot even . . ."

I stop her. "How about I read to you, and you two can sit on your bed."

Her face is still bitter as a cloud, plotting to ruin a picnic on a hot day. I imagine them with this cheesy grin waiting for a family to stroll in the park and set up. It waits patiently to allow them to have one bite each then does its job. It laughs as the family runs away.

Wow, where did that come from?

Doctor Williams gives her medicine and checks on her leg. He is a reliable man. Doctor Williams closes his black leather bag, then whispers to me, "She's doing much better than before, a strong child. However, the infection is spreading fast." He turns and face Ariana and pats her head.

With the doctor's business done, I take Ina out of the room.

"Mama, let's go. Mary Ann getting married remember?" Ina looks more like Mama now with her square face and brown eyes. I can't tell anymore if her round nose is more like Mama's or Papa's. We head down the steps.

Monta is gone and it seems much safer. My sister is out of danger. The same day he shot his step-sister was the same day he left.

Overseers are the same as usual but only one is around most of the time. I'm not sure what happened to Jonathan. Malcolm is long gone, fighting for us. God bless him.

Ina, like always, carries me on and these people have become her family. Rooks are the ones who share what little they have. We don't own a house or a bed to sleep in but what we do have is love. I look after everyone, making sure the young ones behave themselves when the overseers are around. Old woodpecker allows us to get married if we happen to find love.

"Mama, let's go!" She huffs and puffs.

"Okay, okay." I chuckle a little due to her impatience.

Ina runs ahead of me, opening the door. Everyone accumulates around one by one. I hope didn't miss much. Music brightens the evening. We sing and dance.

"Mama," Ina calls.

It never fails. Every time she chimes those words, it makes me remember how it came, almost like a part of me disappeared. I wonder how she would look at me if she called me sister. Would we argue? Tug on one another's hair just out of spite, or maybe hide one another's belongings, get along with no fuss? Sadly, that was stolen from me, a secret buried in the roots and the ashes of Bo and Aunty.

It's a beautiful ceremony. Mary Ann and Amaka are having a blissful day. A couple of words were said then someone tossed out a broom to the ground.

"Mama, what's that for?"

I did not say anything because the best learning situation comes from experience. She's smart, she will figure it out. "I don't know, Ina. Pay attention and you will learn something." Honestly, I didn't know myself.

Mary Ann looks beautiful. Her gown is green. Her smile is big. Her hair is nice and tied back. It's rare seeing her without her maid's head wrap. Amaka is wearing brown trousers and a white long-sleeved shirt with black buttons. His body is chiseled from daily duties. His jaw is sharp like his tone.

The music continues. We are all dancing. I'm dancing with Ina, Mary Ann, Amaka, and everyone else.

"Ina! I'm here." Little Ariana hops her way down her steps.

"Careful, Ariana."

I softly push my sister's head to go dance with her friend. I sit down on a log and view everyone having fun. I feel like Aunty because I am taking care of everyone. I became the person to wash their backs if they should need it, nurse them to health when anyone gets a cold.

"Bloom, you best come dance with me. I'm married," Mary Ann shrieks. She kisses Amaka passionately, her lips devouring his.

I don't have a choice in the matter, so of course, we dance.

Her silly grin compels me to get up while she is snapping her fingers and dances my way. "Abel, you look extra special. Those the same shoes Mistress gave you? I like your yellow dress as well. Spin for me." She twirls me around.

The fun is still alive at night. We make a fire. The wood starts to make a crackling sound. The fire spits out sparks, slowly burning the ground then withering like coal.

"You are so gorgeous, you know that?"

"Child, are you trying to get in my pants? This be me and Amaka's wedding."

I give her a shove of endearment. "Ann!" I sigh. "So happy you found him."

"Stay humble, there is a brighter tomorrow. You know, Abel, the stars do seem brighter." The air feels fresh. "Yeah, it does."

Little by little, color comes to my eyes. I see how the leaves are changing color like a chameleon. Little details like the new home that we are constructing become clear. Thinking like a slave, my happiness dwindles and decays.

"Ina, not too close to the fire now." Amaka picks up Ina and puts her on his meaty shoulders, truly sculpted from the gods.

"Me next, me next." All the children want a turn now.

I cup my hands then shout, "Look what you started, Amaka."

"Mommy, look!" Ariana shouts. The child's soft face reaches Amaka's knee.

April is standing behind me. Her hair tickles my neck, like a soft brush on my skin. She smells like fancy soap. "Thank you for making her happy. She hasn't been herself since the injury." She sits down next to me. It's nice to see this.

"Congratulations Mary Ann." She waves her yellow hat at her. "Did you know she was my midwife? Mary Ann brought Ariana into this world. I suspect the same time as Ina or so."

"Good night, mistress."

I wonder how everyone is back home. I miss my small shed. Everything was in arms reach. Every time I climb Dante's steps, it's like I'm going to heaven. It's a whole maze trying to figure out where items are located.

I miss the cold nights bundled with Mama and Papa. I even miss Mama ruthlessly brushing my hair. I hope they are well. I love you, Mama and Papa.

# Chapter 26

I'm taking my time sweeping the porch. I don't like what I see. Josephine is shaving Jonathan's beard.

"Don't cut me," he barks his order.

She trembles each time the sharp blade teeths at his neck. Imagine your child running with a sharp object. She dips it back in a shallow bowl filled with foam.

"What's taking you so long?" He rolls his eyes at me.

"Almost done," I say. I've been done for a while now. At this point, I'm throwing dust around. In a way, I guess it's dirty. The field is occupied by everyone else, hard at work. Most of the men are shirtless.

Josephine is strong, but she is at her breaking point. I'm afraid she might try something foolish. Her eyes are dazed and there is only the sound of the razor tapping the brim of the bowl. His flesh sinks in while the blade firmly presses down. She carefully strokes up then down. Josephine licks her black lips. It's like Jonathan is testing her and hoping she slips up to give him a reason to excuse his actions.

She dumps the bowl on the side of the creepy statue. "Don't worry, Abel."

I leave the broom leaning on the rails.

Throughout the day, we greet the overseers and Massa with false smiles and bitter tongues that we master to their finest. It's as sharp as a knife that guts pigs.

I love walking in the center of their home. The space is wide and paintings come alive. April's piano downstairs is so lovely. I walk up the stairs to see where my sister is. Unsurprisingly, she is with Ariana. I press my ear against the door.

I hear them giggling. Those two could be sisters, taking me out the picture. I hate thinking as such.

"Yes, who is it? Oh, come in." They are dressed similarly, in pretty white dresses with a flower design in the center.

"Ready, girls? How are you feeling Ariana, Ina?" Both girls respond with "well", which I taught them.

Looks like they are done eating. Small ant-size crumbs are attached to their lips.

"Stay still, Ina." I lick my thumb and smear off any dirt or crumbs then rub my sleeves around her mouth.

"Ma. Gross! Eww. Yuck." Sometimes I wonder if I'm doing the right thing by lying to her, stealing the right to know her family. I can't turn around now. I refuse to explore possibilities.

The girls hop off the bed and are ready for some lessons. I light a few candles. They have a hard time wrapping their minds around what I teach or read to them. I teach them how to write. Dante wants me to spend at least two or three hours with his girl. You were right, Margo. I'm teaching others.

The girls are distracted from hearing music in the other room.

There is not much I can do to reel my two fish back on my hook. "I guess your mother is back, huh Ariana? Here, I'll carry you to her." She nods, showing her gratitude. "Ina, grab her stick for her." Her father built Ariana something to help keep her balance.

"Abel, there you are." Dante approaches me, then commands me to clean his study room. "You girls go on," he says. I head down to his huge room. Still, I am amazed by how rich one person can be.

His study is like a home in itself. His desk is in the middle, made of fine oak. Dante's rack of booze is on the other side. It is a mess in here. Somehow, one of Ariana's shoes locked itself in here. Her shoe is the size of my palm. He usually scolds her about playing in here.

First, I rearrange his chairs, two on each side for whenever he has company. Then, I dust his shelves, even his liquor, though I'm not sure why. I suppose it could get dusty. Behind his desk, I find some documents.

I know what these papers are. To my right is his seal. It's the second time I've had the pleasure to see the keys to my chains. I read Amaka, Mildred, Homer, Abel..

"You know what that is?" Massa asks from the doorway. He gallops in like a proud stallion, a glass above his chest.

"Yes, Massa. Freedom," I say with contentment.

"Let me ask you something, my dear. Why do you think slaves don't run away? I'll tell you why. Because they know the alternative is worse—no life skills, no place to call home. What would you do?"

He paces towards me.

I don't stare but return to dusting.

"Did you see it?" he asks.

"Yes, Massa. Plain as day."

"You know, Abel, I'm sorry. I told myself I'd be a better man than my father was. At least heaven knows I try. He was a bitter fool. I was never into this growing up around him. His tongue was just as foul as his odor. I left home, and I swore I would never come back until my mother wrote me a letter stating she was ill and dying soon. I love my mother. Even though I knew I didn't want to see my father, I dug into that pain and came back here. The plantation, still flocked with slaves, reminded me of the awful sight of my adolescent years. But nonetheless, it was great seeing old friends. Upstairs in my old bedroom, there they were.

"That day, Abel, I still remember like the back of my hand. I guess what I'm trying to portray is, closure. Closure is something we all need." His eyes are glossy. "How was my mother, you ask? She was well, looked like a daisy. It was my father I said good-bye to. She knew I wouldn't have come if she said it was him dying, and he had too much pride. He would not dare write to me. But her lie was forgiven. Not two hours later, he died on my bed. He told me he missed me and to try to be a better man than he was. Our last words are etched in my heart. It was a pleasant welcome. That day I thanked my mother for her heavenly lie that shattered the wall between us. I would have just let the old man pass. They're yours if you want them—the papers for Bo, Antebellum, and Cliff." Dante takes a huge gulp. He makes a hard noise.

I dust the last area on the highest part, a painting of a boat lost at sea. I can barely see the two women figures desperately calling for help. I walk past him with a strong head. "Why don't you burn those as well?"

I go where Mary Ann is cleaning the kitchen. Their kitchen is almost as big as their dining room, with a big circular counter smack in the middle. There is an endless supply of food in every cabinet, plus more in the smokehouse. Mary Ann finishes washing and drying their spoons, knives, and forks.

"You always clean the best, Ann."

"And best not forget it."

That's the last time I give her a compliment.

Everyone else is in their own section, cleaning.

"We should go see if Josephine is okay," I tell her. The house servants' rooms are hidden in the middle corridor.

"Hey, Josephine," we both say. No answer. We wait a second. I hear footsteps of other servants walking around.

"We are coming in." The door is not locked. I just thought I'd be nice and give her some type of respect and courtesy.

"Josephine," I whisper.

"Huh, where you think she be?"

I shrug.

"I don't like this one bit," Ann hollers, rolling her neck.

We search in every room that us house servants are allowed in, but no Josephine.

I run to Ann, out of breath. "I can't find her anywhere!"

From the look on her face, she had been hoping Josephine was behind me. "Abel, let's check outside."

Holding up my dress, we open the Meade's front door like we are raiding a party. "Ann, I don't see her."

"Josephine! Josephine! Benjamin, Patsy, Lonnie, Lamar, Georgia! Ya'll seen where she be?" Nobody can tell us.

"Check the cabin. She has to be in one of those, talking to someone."

We split up again. Not this one, let me check another. Most of the sheds are not far apart from each other. No luck in the next one. I see Mary Ann running in the distance past the tree.

"No, I didn't find her. You check the stables?"

"No, just the outside kitchen." She responds.

"Josephine?" We move toward the back of the stables while the horses start pacing back and forth, pesky bugs cluttering at their tails.

I hear a brushing sound in the back. A faint neigh. It's like a tree that fell is finally lifted off me. "Guys, what's the fuss about?"

"What the fuss about? Abel, you believe her?" In a softer tone, she continues, "What's the fuss about? Got me out here sweating and . . . and cussing. What's the noise about, child I . . ."

"Ann, I fine. Y'all take a swim in a pond or something? Kinda look like that tree out front with its dangling leaves."

We look at one another, exhale, then stupid unknown laughter spills from our mouths.

Night comes in quickly and we prepare food for ourselves and the Meades. I escape into my quarters. Ina is asleep, and I begin to read the letter. Malcolm used a fake name, calling himself Oswald Butler, and it is addressed to April. Smart decision.

# Chapter 27

The cold thrust of December spits itself in. The cold cuts like broken glass. Massa makes sure we are all prepared with blankets and thick fur if necessary. He has to keep his tools in working condition.

I walk into the kitchen after studying with Ina and Ariana.

"Hey, Mildred."

She glares at me with careful alertness. "Anyways, breakfast. You have the first wave, remember? Get to it." She wraps up her scarred arms, even though I already saw the burns.

Dr. Williams comes in today. I watch the doctor's dark carriage approach. He steps out, holding his leather bag.

"Let me take you to her, Doctor," I say. I take him up the left steps. The doctor tells me to leave the room because he has information for the family. Dante and April are in Ariana's small room.

Ina and I are waiting outside the door. The doctor walks out and he takes a sigh. "Dante, I'm sorry. There is nothing more I can do for her. Terribly sorry, old friend."

April walks out. She did not give me any acknowledgment.

I head upstairs in my maid outfit. Ariana wants to speak with me. The child seems forever in pain. She tells me how her foot is rotting, like a hungry dog is constantly gnawing at it.

I barge into Dante's study after talking to his daughter. "What are you doing about Ariana?"

His voice is brimming with empathy. He is sitting down in his dark coat. "I don't know. Make her last moments . . ." He takes off his glasses then wipes his face. "I just don't know."

I don't know either. I head down the corridor to my quarters.

"Come in."

It's Mildred.

"Mildred, listen." I open my desk drawer. I read to her Malcom's letter saying he is okay and still alive. "So he is doing well." She says.

Something troubles her. "Abel, after hearing what you told us, you know, the man that captured you. My story may not be all true."

"What are you talking about?"

Mildred's light hands adjust her head wrap. "For as long I can remember, people never wanted to be around me. My own father left me before I was born. The white lady I mentioned, she told me how I was left behind. She ran into the fiery pits of hell and came after me. Of course, I had to ask if it would have been better to let me die. Then I realized after all those years why she kept an eye on me." She was your mother?" I ask.

"I thought I was some freak. I know my scars make people think twice about approaching me. However, the thing is, she did not know that I knew. It became clear to me. For years now, the only question I ask is why she sell me? I have to find out, but I'm frighten of the answer."

I have no idea what to say to Mildred. What can I say to lift her spirits? What would anyone tell me if they were to hear how my journey to the Meade's plantation came about. "Mildred, I'm so sorry." I rock her shoulder as comfort.

"Don't be. Just look at me. Who want this, born to die? At least my face isn't too bad, right? Well, having no family is better. I don't have to lose anyone. I just wish I knew my Pa."

I take her in my arms. I become closer with Mildred, like my own older sister. Her body is scorched to its flesh, but she is not a cold person. I wonder what went through her father's head to have him do this. Was it the same dark thought that had me succumb to a vile act?

Jonathan has not been around since that night he barged in on Josephine. The chores are the same for me but different for the others. They have more duties raising livestock. They plow the field to prevent any flooding. Women work in pairs, knitting. Most men rebuild outing homes or make new ones. The firewood pile becomes a mountain. We keep the slaughtered animal meat in the smokehouse, adding salt and sugar, sometimes honey, to get it just right.

Mary Ann stays with Amaka outside. She wants to spend time with him.

The cold wakes me up. My head is buried underneath my covers. Two books are on my dresser, halfway read and none completed. I cannot bring myself to finish. Maybe it's the thought that if I get to the end, the book is over. My enjoyment and imagination go with the last words.

I have to paint the missus' nails. Today, she wants red. Of course, she is located where her piano is, never in her room. Monta's room is vacant. Dante locked it. I wonder if will he bring back his son.

"Mistress, it's me, Abel."

April sticks out her toes. They're always done first so she can have more time playing. She is a strange lady.

"Thank you, Abel." Mistress is wearing a thick dark gray jacket with a white bottom.

"Hold still, please. Don't want any on the floor or on you." Her feet are too clean. Almost like she never worked a day in her life. They are smooth with no cracks, no dryness. "Done. Your hand, please." She has soft warm hands compared to me. She might as well shake hands with the bottom of a broom.

"Abel, a few friends are coming over. I'd like to introduce you. They, too, like hearing me play. You might have met one at our brunches. Oh, bring your sister with you."

"Mistress, she is my daughter."

"You don't have to lie. A mother knows. Don't worry. Men are dense. I won't say a word. Although, I'm pretty sure Dante knows. He's a strange man but has a good heart." She winks at me. Mistress smells wonderful.

"Left hand, Mistress." I continue applying red to her nails.

The two girls come in. "Mommy's going to play for you tonight. You know why?" April teases.

Ariana's tiny head rocks, "Yes. My birthday."

"No, not exactly. Today is December second. If you count six more days from now, then it's your birthday. Mommy and Daddy have a surprise for you! But, for today, I want to play with you. Go get dressed for supper, then we will play after. Quickly now."

She hops out of the room, Ina trailing after her.

"I'm grateful for your kindness," I say.

April taps on the piano keys. It makes a high pitch. Corjo would have wanted to meet her. I can imagine Corjo always in awe of her grace. How quickly he would get attached, like I am.

"What's your daughter's age?" I ask.

"She is turning five."

They head downstairs. Ina and myself are following behind like baby ducks. Both of our arms are folded in front of our clothes, walking properly. Ariana begins to fuss because she wants to carry herself down the steps. Persistent one, she is. Each step she takes becomes a struggle. Her efforts are strong, hopping on one leg.

"Let me help you, hon."

The little girl is still refusing her mother's pleading.

Seven steps to go.

"Ariana, be careful." April's face stiffens with worry. Trying to prevent any accidents, her hands are in reach of her daughter dress.

Mary Ann, Josephine, Mildred, Lonny, and two others stand around the table. It's just the family at the table. Dante sits at the head with his wife and daughter on either side.

"Ina, go collect the trash and prepare to wash dishes," Dante demands.

She does not put up a fuss. What could one do if she did? Interfering would make her punishment worse. I've seen them whip the children's arms for disobedience, maybe not Dante, but the others.

The sacrifices the elders make . . . some even lie about broken tools and take the punishment instead. It does not matter if it is their child, they do it for anyone, a bond never to be severed. I will carry the burden so that the sun still shines for her, so that color never fades, and she never questions her existence. It's been eating at me, since the moment they carried me on that wagon. Pa bled on the floor for our sakes, shouting his daughter's name as Ma's long-lasting suffering continued. It strikes me like a loud bell once more. I wonder, who will have it the hardest? Our slave capturer told us.

There are no boys fanning them, so that's good.

By next warm weather, Dante wants Ina out with the rest, but only to collect worms and other small tasks they have the small children do. I tell her everything she needs to know, not that there is a lot. But mainly to stay out of everyone's way.

She told me once that Dante gave her gifts on several different occasions. Ina told me he asked her to report anyone not doing their jobs. I'm glad she told me. I had to tell her who's on her side. I hope Ina knows by now. I did a terrible job instructing her.

"Ina, everyone that looks like you are family, your uncles, aunts, brothers, and sisters. The people that dress nice ain't." I vouched for April and Ina's friend. Otherwise, she will question everything I tell her.

The poor child is coughing dreadfully, looking ill. I can see a red flush through her cheeks. I run to get a damp cloth for Ariana.

"Thank you," she says. Her plate is still full.

"I'll help her to bed, if that's okay?" I ask. I stare at Dante because he is the only parent that might oppose.

"Go ahead. Careful now!" he says, wiping his fingers.

I help her up the stairs. She is too weak to refuse help this time around. The day is still young. She has been tired more recently.

"Sit tight." I run to get another wet cloth and water to drink.

Her head feels hotter than normal. "Does that feel better?"

She hurls out another aching belch.

"Sip this." The glass is empty.

"Abel, it hurts."

Her mother comes in and looks after her. "I brought you a snack," April says.

I close the door helplessly behind me. I walk outside to clear the porch of snow. I can see my breath and I rub my arms, trying to keep warm.

"Abel, get inside." Mildred says.

"Close that door before they holler. I don't want to go back in." She closes the door.

"What troubles you?" Mildred ask.

I drop my hand on the cold rail where the snow thaws. "Everything. I cannot take it anymore, you not knowing your family and me always wondering if mine is okay. Have you ever thought what life would be like if we were free? Sometimes, I wish my skin was white. It makes the most sense."

"At least you lucky. Think about it, if we ever run, you blend real good with the dark, as for me—"

"Shut up."

She breaks into a hysterical laugh. "Come back inside, Abel. Will ya?" I nod my head in disobedience. Just like how Aunty felt, I need to also feel something real. "Can you stay with me for a bit." I ask "I don't want to go back in just yet." She immediately takes hold wrapping her arm around my stomach. "Mildred? Wherever I may end up. I will send a letter to you. Come find me and we will both begin a new journey together."

# Chapter 28

The next day, I am in my quarters. "Ina, make sure you do all your work, then you can play. Study with Ariana if you want."

"Yes, Ma."

I resume my study. When will I be able use the knowledge I obtain while trapped on this plantation?

"Abel, Mistress wants you."

I'm not sure who called me.

Ina and Ariana are cute as ever. The small child begins a hostile cough. Halfway to her Mom, she falls over.

"Ariana, what's wrong?" Ina says.

Ariana does not bother to get herself up or maybe she is not able to.

April scoots out her chair and bends over her child.

"Is it hurting?" April ask.

Her crippled body has to be throbbing with discomfort. "I'm fine, Mommy. Carry me?" She grunts for a few seconds.

"How about this one. You like?" April asks.

The child shakes her head. "Another one, a special piece just for me and my best friend, pretty please." She looks at Ina.

"I hope you and your best friend like this piece."

We applaud every time she finishes playing.

"Another! Another, Mommy." More coughs come in but much more soothing, like the pain is fading. She leans against her mother. They are both in blue dresses.

"Okay, I'll play you my dear friend's favorite song, which I took the time to learn. Hopefully it resembles home."

She looks at me.

Ina tugs on my dress. "What's wrong, Mama? Why are you crying?"

"Shhh, baby."

April begins.

The music blasts me to my past. The music resonates like a newborn child entering life. Then it builds a warm silky cloth around that fits all purposes for its child, comfort, love, praise. While she plays I sense another presence. It leaps out of the bush as a surprise. I can always make you stand on your toes, it says. Then the song cradles its child back to an ever-resting slumber. A voice that ends with I love you.

I want to say something, but my words drift off.

"Another one, Ariana? Hey, baby, just one more. Won't you listen?" Her voice cracks, getting softer. "One more, it's your favorite. Remember when you first heard it? We danced all night. This same time of year, too. Remember how I picked you up and . . . and . . . tossed you around. The way your dress twirled in the air. You . . . you were so concerned about the others. You even told Daddy to let them come inside and warm up and dance with us." Her eyes are red.

I stop her.

All April want is to be alone. She never steps back into her piano room. Dante's tone is not cold, nor does he take it out on us slaves. His subtle command makes you think otherwise. We do whatever we can until Aril and Dante heals. Both of them are dealing with the loss of their daughter differently.

I make April soup. I hope she likes it. It's my only specialty.

I tap on her door. "Mistress, I have something for you." I push the door open.

Her nose is red and running. It's been at least two weeks since they saw their child.

I don't want to experience what she is going through again.

April takes the soup, managing to say thank you.

I watch as she gently blows at steam. It fights back, only becoming cool after four blows. What should I say?

"Enjoy. Anything else?"

In a faint tone, she says, "No, that will be all, Abel."

December 20th.

Mistress packs up her bags. "Grab that, Abel hon. Maybe my black dress and the gray one as well."

"The one that makes it look like you can't breathe? Have your chest perky?"

"They are all like that, my dear. Grab my purple shawl in the closet. Also, my hat. It's hung on the nail over there."

Mistress is doing much better. April is going to visit her parents, to get away from the big house. I will see her when the snow stops falling.

"Don't forget your scarf. Stay warm."

April is looking like a fool trying to pack. She is tripping on her solid black dress.

"Mistress, your ride here," Lonny says. Lonny keeps to herself. She wants nothing to do with most. She doesn't hate anyone, just doesn't want to be bothered. Lonny is a dark-skinned, middle-aged woman. Her hair is nearly gray and shriveled. She is in-between big and skinny. Lonny shines with service and posture.

I peek outside the window. There is a lantern attached to the stagecoach.

"Bye, Abel. Bye, all. Bye, Dante."

We wave at the missus. It's good seeing her happy. There is too much sadness. We don't need her in the mix.

I spend most of the winter in the house. I go outside only a few times to see Ann.

Ina still misses her friend but, like April, she is doing much better.

"Ina, are you ready for your lesson?"

"Mama how long we staying here?" It is an honest question with no answer.

"Not sure. Till people wake up."

She starts fidgeting whenever she does not know an answer to my questions. Just like how I was tapping my feet. I only wish she knew the other children better. Ina spent most of her time with Ariana.


January 15th.


I'm awakened by a jumping child on my stomach.

"She back. She back."

I quickly get out of bed to greet the mistress.

In the back of her wagon is a device. "What's that, April?"

"This is called the cotton gin. It should make life easier for all."

"I'm sure everyone will appreciate the nice gesture, but why?"

I see she did more than just visit her parents. She is radiant with a confident energy. Her yellow hat matches her blouse.

"I'm tired of being looked down on. It is time for me to help. I cannot take credit. It was her birthday wish, trying to help however she could. If there ever is anything I can do for you, just ask." April whistles for a couple of men to help her.

Massa is having a big party in a couple of days. He is running for something. I just don't know what it is. There's a lot of fuss buzzing about, so it might be crucial.

Ann returns to her room. Massa is always fond of her help and the knowledge she has to hold down his home.

We gather in the kitchen to clean. Josephine's emotions sway from content to worry. She is quiet while Mildred gets louder.

"Don't forget to place the dishes in the right place, Ina," Mildred tells her.

"Guess what, ya'll?" Ann says.

"What?" the whole tribe asks.

"Okay, since there's young around, I ain't saying much, but Mama got a child coming!"

"Congrats," I say.

Mary Ann turns. "Child, get off me, ain't no kicking from the baby just yet."

"Oh sorry, it's just, I did that when Ma had Ina."

"Sorry Abel, I did not mean it like that. We could use more family, huh girls?" She walks to Josephine. "Can you get the stored meat? Early preparation. Besides I'm afraid these two knuckleheads will mess up." Mildred and I smile with content of not doing more chores.

She bounces her way through. I have to admit Josephine looks the silliest in this outfit. The color might not suit her.

I go around dusting. Mildred and Ina take care of the trash around the house. The others are upstairs cleaning, dusting, folding.

"Abel, remember now, this party different from his usual dinner which only has a few people," she shouts across the room.

Josephine comes back. It's hard to pay attention to what she says. My mind starts dreaming. I hear her but do not comprehend her words. Whenever she asks any question, I just hope everyone else is listening then I can ask them later.

It's getting dark. I return to my quarters with Ina. I hope the cotton gin is working out nicely. "Ina, go wash up and get ready for bed."

"Tell me a story." She says inching toward me, her feet cold as ice.

"Long ago, there was a cute child, a girl. She stayed in a big house with so many windows. Each window fascinated this child. Each window was filled with, um, pigs."

"Pigs? Mama, this story terrible."

"Well, it's hard coming up with something good, not like I do it. Well, the pigs are colored white, black, and Friday."

"Ain't that a day, not a color, Mama?"

"Keeping you on your toes. Back to the story now. Quit interrupting or you will never know what happened to the pig called Ina."

"What happened?! Tell me," she demands.

"I don't know. Guess we'll find out. The three pigs are close friends but belong to me. I treat them kindly."

"What you do to them?" she asks. Her face like a shadow.

"I bathe them and feed them real nice. So, one day-"

"What are the other two names?"

"Your pig comes up to me and you know what I did?"

"Forget to name them . . ."

"No, I ate that pig. It was delicious, had plenty of leftovers. Pig feet are scrumptious. The end. Blah!" I start to tickle her toes and stomach, an aching shriek bellowing from her.

"I want to tell the next story. Long ago, um, people learn how to live uh . . . on the clouds. Yeah, clouds. There was a mama, a papa, and two suns."

"Sun or son?"

"Mama, don't stop me. I did not to you."

My jaw drops. "Sorry," I say.

"The suns are the key, one of them fell out the clouds. He be clumsy one. He learn the ways of the ground people then, then . . . then." She takes a big yawn.

"Ina, Ina! What became of the sun? What did he do?" I have to wake her.

Her cold toes wrap around my thighs. I roll over so we are eye to eye. She looks deliciously at peace. Her frizzy hair is over her nose. It twitches as she scratches. Ina turns her back. It doesn't matter where we are, as long as we connect.

# Chapter 29

"How the fish coming along?" Ann shouts, trying to get everything else in order. Her head is greasy. "Make sure the chicken is good and ready. Hurry up, people. Only a few more hours! Who making tea? Best not make it too sweet nor bitter. Gotta be just right, like myself. Don't burn anything, Abel!"

Always picking on me.

"Yes Ma'am." I'll just go have Ina help me set the table. "Ina can you help me?"

"Uh-huh."

We are leaving the food on the table, so the guests can eat at any time.

"Sit the bread there, maybe move the candle over here. Careful, it looks fancy. Don't drop it, Ina." I scout the place like a hunter, doing a last-second check.

I stand by the door. A swarm of guests floods his home. Wealth stains their smiles. Dante gives us fresh clothes, making sure we resemble his wealth.

I'm standing in the corner with Ina. All I see are fresh whips. It's a noisy evening filled with music, white people, and more white people.

"Abel, have you seen Josephine?" Mildred asks.

"No. Go ask Ann or maybe Penny. We been here for the most part."

Dante's spoon hits his glass. "Ladies and gentlemen, may I have your undivided attention . . ."

"I cannot find her!" says Mildred.

"Did you check her room?"

She says no.

"I'd like to thank you all for attending my ceremony."

She grabs me and pulls me away from the crowd of pale skin and silk dresses to the middle narrow corridor. "Josephine, Josephine," we whisper.

"Maybe she went to get more liquor," Mildred wheezes out.

Mildred and I take a step outside the horde of people.

"She is taking an awful long time getting drinks," I say.

The screech that comes from our mouths could pierce an eardrum after opening the door to where we store extra bottles.

"Josephine, Josephine!" Her breasts are exposed.

My tone is soft. "Josephine, why?" It looks like a small storm went through the room, one that left blood, broken bottles, and a helpless woman.

"Go get Ann, please."

My friend dangles in front of me.

"Josephine! Lawd, no don't take my baby." Ann comes from behind her. "Lawd, no, no." Her face is hot like peppers. "I just saw him too, the smile of satisfaction he had. I don't care, I don't care! Mildred, can you get Amaka for me? Help with Josephine."

"That man, I'll hurt him" she shouts, pacing about. "That man to blame, not my poor child. Lawd, not another." Ann is heading outside to the door.

"Ann, stop. You cannot do it. They will hurt you, take you from us. Let me try something," I plead with exhaustion like a slave wanting freedom. "We cannot have you beaten or sold, or worse, so I beg you, don't go inside."

She is not listening, her hands reaching for the door. "Abel, I'm sorry but I don't care what happens to me."

"What about Amaka?" I say. I'm not sure what more I can say but her fingers pause at the knob. She plummets to her knees.

"Abel, she was like my daughter. She never really had any family."

"Think about Amaka," I repeat.

"I preached that I would help her with him. What good am I if I don't?" She stands up and clutches the broken glass, opening the door. The music hits us like a wave.

"He will understand." Her mind is frozen with anger.

The room brims with laughter and drunk people. By the door, there are huge tables with sandwiches and drinks. Candles are around the table. The air is sweet.

A mother's wrath is sour.

Jonathan is easy to spot, scarfing down a plate of food. The broken bottle is hidden in her small pouch. She is blind with rage. Whatever transpires, she is willing to risk everything.

What should I do?

"Ann, if you do this, I will run away. And I hope I get caught. I'll be beaten. I hope they rip my clothes off, too. If you don't care, think about that." I do not yell but it is enough to make her stomach turn.

"What business do y'all have with me?"

She freezes.

"Congrats, congratulations. Dante, a toast for your campaign. I hope it does not fail this time."

"Ann, we should leave." I say over the loud applauds and screams of congratulations.

She is trembling. I can tell she still yearns to drive the glass through him.

Josephine is buried on Sunday. Off in the distance. We would have done the same for Aunty, Bo, and Cliff.

Lawd, another rook. Come one, come all. Josephine, all she ever wanted was to be surrounded with her family. Poor girl done nothing but survive, yet deprived of life. No mistake on her part, no blame shall shame her. We still alive. Lawd, we thank you for that and much more. We still alive but with each kin the bond we share only becomes stronger. Never lose sight, Josephine. Your family will thrive. -Amen-

"Mama, will you be okay?" she asks, squeezing my arm.

"Eventually, Ina. Eventually."

There is only one course left to take.

I find the mistress in her room, glaring at her piano. Her gloved hands are folded behind her back.

"I humbly ask that you find a way to get rid of Jonathan without asking why, please."

She turns around. "Abel, what . . ."

"Please, I ask of this one favor. If you don't, nothing good will happen with the servants."

"I have to tell Dante. Plus, we. You know what consider it done."

"Thank you." She is definitely a new woman.

"Wake up, Ina. Go help the other children." The child can sleep till the next day at times.

"Mama, did you go somewhere last night?"

"I couldn't sleep so I got up from the bed is all." She does what I do, making sure Mama doesn't go anywhere. "Run off now."

# Chapter 30

Summer of 1865

I'm announced a free woman.

We celebrate all night.

Malcolm never did come back, but I hope all is well. None really have a place to call home. They have known this plantation like a learned pain. Dante gives us all the option to stay and work, with housing and food for minimal earning.

Only I decide to leave. I say my farewells.

"Apple." Mary Ann teases "thank you for what you did to get rid of that awful man. These two would not be in my arms right now." Mary Ann holds her babies, twins in fact, a boy and girl. Josephine and Toby.

April escorts Ina and me home by train.

The train whistle sounds as a gush of black smoke purges out. April leads the way to our seats. I sit by the window. April is across in a white blouse.

"Ina, something I have to tell you—a truth I've been holding back from you since you were young." I never thought I get a chance to tell her.

She looks at me with an acute expression that makes me hesitate.

"Yes, Mama?"

I can't believe we survived. I go into minor detail. I couldn't bare to tell her everything.

"My sister?"

I nod, then kiss her on her soft cheek.

Just a little longer, guys. Wait for us.

The train ride is much smoother and faster than wagons, that's for sure. Mistress and I talk while Ina is taking a nap.

"Ina, hey Ina, wake up. We're here."

Stepping outside, we call for a ride. The air feels and smells familiar. My sleeves are drenched in drool. Her first act of sisterhood is struck. She takes a huge yawn. Ina is missing her front tooth.

The town is tasteless. I might have spotted Tommy from those mean kids. He's on a roof hammering. He looks more mature and handsome plus it appears his hammer has chiseled him.

We ride through. I notice more buildings destroyed. If I make a left, I'll be at Corjo's house. Oh, how I want to see him so badly. Soon Abel, soon.

The red fence is not far from view. "We here. We here. I shout. I'm carrying our bags.

"Mama, is that it?"

I place my free hand over my mouth in awe. "Yes. Yes, it is. Hold my hand now."

"Remember, Abel, we leave in three days," April shouts from the wagon.

The giant tree has been chopped. I check in the shed for old time's sake. No one is in here.

"Mama, what are you doing?" Ina tugs on my dress.

"Call me Abel, Ina. I'm just remembering."

I take a long whiff. Ah, it smells wonderful. The shed feels like a matchbox after living under the roof Meades plantation.

The bench is there. Everything looks intact

"Ina, ready to see Mama and Papa?" I'm eager. "Race you to the door." I drop the bag.

She trails behind me, but her small legs can't keep up.

I bang on the door. "Mama, Papa."

She repeats after me, "Papa, Mama." Well, almost.

The door opens. I thought I would have seen them sitting down.

I echo once more, "Mama, Papa? It's me, Abel. I'm home.
Flies hover above on the counter. The room is dim.

I turn my head towards the hallway. There he is. "Papa!
Papa!" Pa is thin as paper. His rib cage pierces through his dry
skin. His arms are like strings.

I run at him. "Pa!"

"Abel?"

"Papa."

"My beautiful daughter! And who is that behind you?"
He starts sniffling. "Is that Ina?" Pa Looks at me. "Is that my
baby?" He ask. He approaches her. "Hello" He says softly.

"Where's Ma? She sleeping?"

I run down the short, narrow hallway, jerk my head through
their room, but she isn't there.

"Ma!" I think she is in the bathroom. "Mama, I'm home." I
have this big stupid smile.

"Pa, where's Mama? Is she getting firewood?"

His face is still and it tells the grim truth.

"Papa, where's Mama?" My voice shrivels.

He does not say a word.

I dart past him to see if Mama is carrying firewood. My
whole body swings backwards into his before reaching the
door. "No. Let go of me." I try to break free. "No, no. Pa let
go!" I start attacking Pa. He lets me pound at his chest.

"Mama not here?" Ina asks.

"She got sick like me, but..." He can't finish his sentence.

"Mama?" Ina says. "Mama? where is she? You said I could meet her! I want to ask her so much. Like can we cook together, oh, oh...I want to tell her my favorite food and maybe..." Ina's voice is sour.

What else can I say?

"Mama?"

If she say it one more time, I swear I'll...

"Mama?"

Papa picks me up, then Ina, and just holds us. I feel like a stack of wet paper, slipping through his arms and melting to the floor.

Visions of her flash through my head. My body is weak as I merge into his arms.

"My beautiful daughters, I'm so sorry. Forgive me for not taking better care of you. Forgive me for not protecting your Ma!" His grip tightens.

I'd rather face a hundred lashes than face this. It burns.

I can't sleep. I stay up all night, tossing and turning until I awaken. I walk to the bench in the middle of the night.

"I knew you be out here," Pa says. His cheeks are bony. "I come out here every night." He sits close to me.

"It still hurts, Papa."

"I know. She loved you so much, Abel. She couldn't bear it. If I wasn't so weak..."

I hug Pa.

"I had nights that I cried myself to sleep. Nights that I couldn't sleep. Awful nights that brought me to my knees, praying...begging for my daughter's return. Not just for me; your Mama really needed you. I prayed till morning. I come out here thinking about you, wondering, is she still writing? Are her wings broken? Are you upset with me, Abel?"

I tap him how Mama used to if he ever asked a stupid question.

The next day, I decide to see if Corjo is home. "Ina, come with me. Pa, I'll be right back."

"Big sis, where are we going?"

I look down at her with a shy smile. "To see my friend. He is not like us, but he is so nice. I promised him one day you and him would meet."

"Just like you said I meet Mama?"

She didn't mean to wound me. I see his house.

Bang, bang, bang. Three quick bursts and nothing more. Corjo, Corjo.

"Why are you smiling like that, sis? You look kinda red on your cheeks, too. How you do that?"

"Shh. No, I'm not."

She starts doing something. I suppose trying to change color.

The door opens, revealing a round belly in a red plaid shirt. "How can I help you?"

It is his father. I take a huge step back, putting Ina behind me. On his cheek is a healed cut.

"Do I know you? Just because slavery over, don't expect me to be friends with you people."

"Wait a minute." Mr. Jones' eyes got wide. "You look familiar. You're that girl from, what, six years ago? I'm sorry for what I've done and–"

"Dad, who is it?" Corjo says. He is wearing jeans and a black shirt. His skin is like copper. Corjo is more chiseled and lean, not like before. On his face is facial hair but nothing significant. Corjo's hair is short and split like the ocean.

"Hello, Corjo" I say. He closes the door behind his father.

"Do I know you?"

"Stop kidding around. I'm really happy to see you! A lot has happened."

He looks to his left down the street then the opposite direction.

"It's me, Abel."

He stares at me blandly. "How do you know my name?"

I start to boil with anger. "We swam in the river, ate food at Connie's Joint. Remember? People are such idiots." I chuckle nervously. I want to hear so much about him.

"I guess they are. Well, pardon me, Abel." I smash my finger when he attempts to close the door on me. "Are you serious, Jones? Stop acting the fool."

"Who are you? Look, we don't have any money."

I begin to rant. "Chess! Milo."

"Go away, please!" I back away.

"Sis, he is a big meany."

The door closes behind him and nothing else is said. I bang on it one more time.

I repeat my actions. "Corjo! Please don't forget about the times we had. I need you..." Each desperate word is like a slicing blade.

"Abel, you okay?"

I'm not sure how to respond. "Let's go home."

On our way back home, I get lost in my head. Is it my fault? If you are truly real, like they say, send me a sign or forever be forgotten by me. Would you even care?

I look back before I'm too far, but only a trail of dirt follows. I ask once more, who am I to you?

Corjo doesn't know my name nor my face, so what does that make me? A ghost of his past—a figment that never existed.

"How is Corjo? I haven't seen him in a long time, almost like he forgot about me," Pa asks.

We sit on the sofa.

"He was a meany, Papa. Didn't even say hi!" Ina puffs her lips together, reminding me of Ma.

"Sorry about Corjo. He helped me and Ma so much. Brought us medicine and food. Such a great kid."

"I don't want to talk about him, Papa." I almost forget to tell Papa about April. So I begin to tell him.

"April is what you might say, my Margo."

# Chapter 31

I go to see where Ma is buried. She is right behind the shed. I see sticks and shriveled flowers. I want to say goodbye to my best friend. I sit down.

"Bye, Ma. Thank you for everything you did for this family, especially me. It wasn't easy living how we did, but we made it work, right? We never fought but we did argue. I suppose I did most of the yelling, huh? Sorry about being so stubborn and annoying. If you were to glance through that toy shop, what would you want?

"You know why I always kept my cold feet on you, Ma? I had to make sure you were still there. Every movement or toss in your sleep, I had to know. I slapped Pa's face as well. Funny—you both knew, didn't you? What I'm trying to say is thank you for being there.

I need you. You know that. In the end, I'm the one who went away. Sorry, Ma. It seems I cannot stop my tears from attacking you.

"Your daughter Ina is so beautiful, Mama. She's probably a younger you. I wish you were here to watch her bloom into an educated woman. She's creative, that's for sure. Her toes are cold, too. Every night, she never was an inch from me.

How annoying, huh? The best part of my life was knowing you picked my name. I know it's not possible, but can we lie and say I heard you? Please? Just this once.

"I might have appeared strong, but I hated not hearing your voice. Mama, my heart feels heavy. The pain, the pain runs through my entire body. Ma, if you were to burn a bundle of paper could you put back the ashes as a whole? May I see your smile just once more? Don't take this the wrong way, but I pray that I had it the hardest. I'm lost for words and you know my mouth is like a vault.

"Sorry, Mama. These ignorant tears keep ruining my thoughts. They just won't stop. I'm wiping and wiping but—oh Ma, help me. Why can't I stop? I taste it in my mouth. It's so salty. Now my nose, Ma. I can't breathe, Mama. I can't breathe! Ma! What should I do? I'm drowning.

"Ma, I need to know something. What's your name? I need to see your face just once more. If I don't, what does that make you?"

"Abel! Abel! What are you doing?" Papa said.

"She's not meaningless, Pa! What's her name?"

"Abel, don't. You know her name."

"I don't know your name, Ma.

Pa carries me on his shoulder even though he's weak. The back of his shirt is moist with feelings. Ina is lost in the noise. It's a side of me she hasn't seen. The youth that vanished, a daughter.

He sets me on the sofa. I cry myself to sleep.

I run through the shed. The tin tub is still standing in the corner. The mattress is filled with leaves.

I dust off the book and I look inside. I begin to scan through: catch up, are you writing about me? Fingers interlock, it might be a bumpy ride. It brings back memories. I see chapters I never wrote.

I sit down and read through The Harvest. It looks like a piece was ripped out.

Corjo added a few chapters about me. He even goes to say, "Guess what, Captain? I'm always loyal. I told you I would read it to the world and I intend to. I do miss you. Now that I'm grown, I know what I want."

Pa walks in. "Yes, Pa."

I steal the book. I pack what I can find in Margo and Ma's belonging.

"Abel, I need a quick nap. I'm feeling a bit tired. But before that. Remember the story I always told Ma?"

"Yes, Papa. Like a ritual. Should I say it?" His eyes slowly close. He exerts deep breaths. He starts to cough harshly. "Please. Ina, listen to your sister. Go ahead."

There is a subtle peck on the back door. Kraa kra kaaw. On the porch is the same scarred raven. Kraa kaw. It flaps its majestic ink dried wings but never takes flight or shows fear even after I try to startle it away. Behind it is queen chess piece. Both white and black queen chess pieces. "Abel, Pa still sleeping. Papa? Papa!"

"Ina! Let him rest. I will be right back." A stupid thought comes to me.

"But Abel, he not..."

I cut her off. "Tell April to wait! I won't be long." I slam the door behind me and grab what I need.

I bolt to Corjo's house and the raven follows me, then perches on his rooftop. He answers, and I beg him to play.

"Look, why don't you leave me alone or I will call the sheriff."

"One game and after this I will leave you alone, I promise. I will not leave until you decide to play me. Please, I can give you money, win or lose okay?"

"Fine, I just want you gone." His arms cross.

I set the game up. "White or black pieces?" I ask.

After Dante's son tormented my sister I couldn't stand to look at another board. Why am I doing this?

I move my queen. "This used to be our favorite game, even if you don't remember. I can't give up just yet. I'm persistent, remember?"

"Me and you, friends? I highly doubt that, sorry. After this, keep your coins and leave."

I agree with his terms. "I didn't have money anyways, sorry."

He smirks. The craters on the sides of his cheeks comes in.

We are still fierce, trying to outwit each other. Pawns for pawns. Then he throws his queen at me, dominating my side until I vanquish her with my queen. Both perish.

"Close game."

I wish it was sweat rolling across our skin.

"It's raining and getting cold." He says looking at his shirt.

"Not yet. Stay. It's only a small drop." I'm moving my hair out of my eyes every second. The rain becomes too much.

He says, "Okay, this is annoying. Sorry."

"Wait, please one more. He closes his door.

For once, the weather mimics my mood. The rain drops hard.

I absorb the sensation of the heavy rain. How would he remember me? I'm not the same girl he knew. I don't have the same hopeful eyes.

Not far down the road, sounds of sloshing and splashes draw near me. I feel a quick jerk on my arm, then my hips whirl around.

"Destiny."

You know my name and you know my face, so what does that mean?

"A face without a name is intangible, as is a name without a face."

# About the Author

Franklin Neal was born in Liberia and moved to the states at a young age.

He has always wanted to tell emotional and powerful stories. Rooks of the Raven is his debut novel and he hopes to write many original stories for his fans to enjoy.

# Acknowledgement

I would like to show my gratitude towards my family and friends who helped shape my story. My outstanding launch team for all their contribution. Another appreciation to Self-Publishing School. Without them, I would not have made it this far. And lastly, special thanks to Sylvia Ellis and Maurice Dyson who were the first to read Rooks of the Raven my debut novel.